SAR

ALL THE CHARACTERS
IN THIS BOOK ARE
FICTITIOUS
INCLUDING
THE
AUTHOR

Sarah Binks

PAUL HIEBERT

Introduction by A. Lloyd Wheeler

General Editor: Malcolm Ross

New Canadian Library No. 44

MCCLELLAND AND STEWART

The Canadian Publishers
McClelland and Stewart Limited
25 Hollinger Road, Toronto
0-7710-9144-3

Manufactured in Canada by Webcom Limited

SONNET

When I have turned life's last descriptive page,
And written *finis* to a somewhat unplanned tale,
With here its moments of poetic rage,
And there long prose of dubious avail,
My friends will come and say, "He was a sage,
Lo, count the leaves, in truth, 'tis noble, look!
All this accomplished in his single age!"—
And sigh, and reverently close the book:

But from the multitude will come a few,
Sweet sprightly souls who read not to enlarge
Each chapter to heroic tome, nor view
The title page as bright emblazoned targe—
But lovingly, to thumb each page anew,
And chuckle at the doodles on the marge.

A Dedication

"After all, what was the beauty of sky and field and rain-drenched hill, of prairie swept by storm, of dazzling alkali flat, of hot fallow land in the sun of the summer afternoon, of the misty pastels of spreading-time? All these things had been hers ... but she knew that they could never be completely hers, that they belonged to the prairie and to the West—that they were of Saskatchewan for all time."

"Come drought, come rust, come high tariff and high freight rates and high cost of binder twine—and what about the roads—I still say to you as I have already said to the electors of Quagmire and Pelvis, that a Province that can produce such a poet may be down but it's never out."

To those of the West who have seen these things and endured these things, who have known the round of what Sarah calls "The Four Seasons," and have lived bravely—through good times and bad—this book is affectionately dedicated by the Author.

Introduction

WHEN asked how *Sarah Binks* came into being, Paul Hiebert used to say something like this: "You know at an afternoon tea, you soon exhaust the weather as a topic of conversation. Then, to avoid an awkward pause, you ask, 'Have you heard Sarah's latest poem?'" And so the poems were accounted for. When his listeners began to ask, "Who is Sarah?" Hiebert supplied biographical details. Whether strictly true or not, Hiebert's account explains how knowledge of and interest in Sarah Binks, the Woman and the Poet, began to spread on the campus at Manitoba and in the city of Winnipeg. For Hiebert's colleagues, singly or in small groups, Sarah relieved the tedium of a long ride to the Fort Garry site of the university in a lurching Winnipeg streetcar. And soon Sarah Binks as presented by Paul Hiebert became the evening's topic at meetings private and public. For several successive years Hiebert was on the program of the student English club. I recall student lungs crowing like chanticleer on these occasions, especially at some high spot like Sarah's "almost perfect" translations from the German:

> Me is as if the hands I
> On head yours put them should.

These performances involved more than the spread of Sarah's fame. During this period of Sarah's gestation—before she was born into print—Hiebert was testing and revising his work. He could judge its effectiveness under various conditions, with individuals, with groups formal and informal, and with audiences of different kinds. I do not mean that he measured his success by mere volume of laughter but rather that he presented his work under conditions which kept demanding a fresh appraisal. He was following the Horatian injunctions to delay publication and to polish. Finally the diverse ingredients, the broad, the wild, the flat, the inflated, the crude, the naughty, the ribald, and the grotesque, all made their appropriate contributions to the planned total effect.

In *Sarah Binks* we have both a critical biography of the poet, which may for convenience be called the Life, and her poetical works, the Letters. The Life subserves the Letters. By merely *spacing* the poems the prose increases their effect. If piled in a heap, these semi-precious stones might look like pebbles. As it is, each poem has its own setting, and the reader has a chance to appreciate its quality.

But the Life has its own value too. I intend later to discuss it as a prose counterpart of Hiebert's Hudibrastic verse, a burlesque of literary biography. This, however, is only one of its artistic features. Comic incongruity can operate in every aspect of human activity. And the field of fire of Hiebert's satirical guns is a wide arc. To select a few items, it sweeps from Canadian culture through politics, education, rural life and urban sentimentalizing of rural life, to human quirks and oddities. The whole incident of the Wheat Pool Medal and the publication of Sarah's poems in *Swine and Kine* will illustrate the first. Education will be illustrated later. The story abounds in comments on farming and rural life, but the city dweller's sentimentalizing of them emerges most clearly in such poems as *The Song of the Chore*, *The Farmer and the Farmer's Wife* and *Song to the Four Seasons*. Human oddities appear not only in the main characters but also in the minor ones, even those referred to only in footnotes. As for politics, Windheaver opens the story with his complacent remark, "I think I was wise to leave out the tariff in my speech." His complaints about the roads become a recurrent theme. This theme Hiebert modulates into Mound Builder at one point to sharpen the effect:

> My friends, there is a big difference between building a mound and throwing up a heap of dirt. (Cheers.) I say this to you about Afflatus; he will be building them upside-down next. (Loud laughter.) And what about the roads! What about the mounds if there is no road to get to them!

This passage illustrates not only the nature of Hiebert's material but also the liveliness with which it is presented. Life breathes through the book from the first scene when, according to Windheaver, "It was hot as hell!" to the concluding word, "Alone." Even such a small detail as the names Hiebert gives to people and places deserves notice, for they are not always obvious; sometimes, as in Greenglow, they have a subtle Dickensian fitness. They also reflect Hiebert's fertility of invention. In one debauch he lists, "Quagmire, Pelvis, Detour, Hitching, Quorum, Baal, Vigil, Oak Bluff, and Cactus Lake," and he then proceeds to mention five more. His attitude to his characters is ambivalent, as it is to English words and poetic genres; he loves them while he mocks them. And perhaps because of his affection, once he has set Ole, Mathilda, "Old Sage" Thurnow, and the rest in motion, they seem to perform their antics of their own volition. The town of Willows, too, though not as substantial as W. O. Mitchell's Crocus, nevertheless casts a long shadow in the Saskatchewan morning sun.

As a critical biography *Sarah Binks* meets the standard requirements. Hiebert duly notes the influences on Sarah: Ole, Rover, Henry Welkin, and others. He traces themes and images to their proper sources: by his efforts the geological vein in Sarah's verse is laid open to view. He reveals his concern to establish the canon of Sarah's works, describing his research in the Introduction and elsewhere. Furthermore he frankly admits the limits of his research. "There is no doubt," he writes, "that some of Sarah's finest work still lies buried among the Tax Sales and Mortgage Foreclosures." He freely admits the weakness of the early poems in such statements as the following: "her rhyming of 'visible' with 'contemplation' is not in the best traditions of Saskatchewan literature." He acknowledges the work of other critics and assesses their judgements. He himself is scrupulous in recording an authentic text but does not pretend that all his predecessors have been irresponsible. Miss Rosalind Drool has let her imagination run away with her and in her misguided zeal has added verses of her own to one of Sarah's poems in *Up From the Magma*, and so it is difficult, "according to Professor Marrowfat, 'to decide which is Binks and which is Drool.'" For good measure we have oblique reflections of the Baconian cipher in the Binks–Thurnow controversy and of the natural tendency of biographers to divide a writer's life into periods, in Sarah's case the Pre-Regina and Post-Regina years, or P.R. and P.R.

Behind both the content and technique of any work and as important as general vitality lies the "kind of awareness" of the author. In Hiebert's case it is critical perception, a clear view of the "discrepancy between the ideal and the fact" or more simply of the incongruous. The distinctive quality of this faculty in Hiebert can be illustrated by this story that he bequeathed to his colleagues upon his retirement from the university. "When I go into my second-year Chemistry class and say, 'Good morning,' they reply, 'Good morning.' When I go into my *fourth*-year Chemistry class and say, 'Good morning,' they write it down." The underlying critical perception is manifest, but so is the ability to present the satiric point, deftly phrased, in a telling situation. This critical perception, or satiric vision, controls the whole work, both Life and Letters. I ignored it when in my first section I said that the diverse ingredients, the broad, the wild, the grotesque made their appropriate contributions to the whole. They did so because they were directed and controlled by Hiebert's critical intelligence.

Hiebert's comment on the benefits of a Science course just quoted when placed beside a passage in *Sarah Binks* illustrates his free movement from comedy to farce and the range of tone in his work from the sober to the riotous, from the restrained to the wild. The passage deals with William Greenglow's record at St Midget's College:

> According to his own records ... he had obtained a total of ten and a half units, fourteen credits, eleven and five-sixteenth pundits during the first term of the second half of the first division, and by transferring three digits from the diploma course ... he would have a total of twenty-three half-credits, which would entitle him to the degree of Jack of Arts, leaving six marklets, or one semi-microbe, which could later be counted towards the degree of Bachelor of Arts.

In the days of Sarah's infancy Hiebert used to declare, "It is hard to write a good bad poem." There is no better lead to the heart of Sarah's poetry than 'good bad''. The bad inheres in the good and by Hiebert's artistry becomes good. In *Henry IV*, Hotspur describes a parallel procedure: "out of this nettle, danger, we pluck this flower, safety."

Just as the Life satisfies the requirements of critical biography so the poems satisfy the requirements of poetry. First of all the poet must show that he loves and cherishes words. Hiebert writes of Eagle Feather,

> Gone from his *quoin* 'til his days are counted. [Italics mine.]

And the poet must, as Hiebert does here, combine the evocative word with a haunting cadence. On the other hand artistic fitness occasionally demands the orderly march and steady beat of accents; these we find in the lines,

> And what we spread will once more come to view.

> And he who walks with criss-cross gait
> Can read the cosmos like a slate.

Again, content and technique must be fused. The following line not only contains the striking word *shrill* but also exemplifies the power, necessary to an artist, to distil a dramatic situation into a single verse:

> Thy voice has lost its shrill.

We are indeed fortunate that it is Hiebert who brought out the definitive edition of Sarah's work. He thereby rescued her poems from the profane hands of Miss Rosalind Drool, Dr Taj Mahal, and Horace P. Marrowfat. The extent of our debt can be estimated if we imagine these critics in operation on some of Sarah's finest lines. Taj Mahal, with his mathematical obsession, would probably find in this line,

> Tut! Whistle low, with peakered beak,

nothing but an objectionable departure from the norm of the iambic tetrameter metre. Miss Drool's excesses have already been noted, and her interpolation of her own frustration complexes need not detain us here. Marrowfat is all too ready to fall into the muskeg of the "personal estimate" as we see in this comment: "But I know just the feeling Ole has. I have it myself almost every Saturday night." It is hard to say how many poems he might have suppressed on crude moralistic grounds, and we might, were it not for Hiebert, have lost the ringing assonance of the line

> But beans alone appease desire.

But to argue thus is to take windmills for giants. It would be better to use a valid criterion. Coleridge proposed, as the "infallible test of a blameless style," "its untranslatableness in words of the same language without injury to the meaning." If we apply this canon to the following lines, what do we find?

> And send out the S. O. L. my hearties,
>
> And call back Cincinnatus to the plough,
>
> He knows not life, the one who never ever,
> Has burned the midnight coal-oil in his time.

Answers will vary. But the test brings out one fact clearly: that Hiebert exploits incongruity in both diction and idea. We can say, also, that if these lines are not strictly "untranslatable," they are nevertheless unique. Moreover they clearly indicate that when Sarah asked the following question,

> This makes me scratch myself and ask,
> When shall my powers fade?

she was reflecting merely the scope of her speculation.

Earnest readers of *Sarah Binks* may welcome the suggestion that, in order to enhance the charm of Sarah's work, her poems be classified as Wordsworth did with his in the 1815 edition. I offer a few suggestions. Pastoral: *The Farm Skunk, Spreading Time*; Descriptive: *Wash Out on the Line*; Elegiac: *Eagle Feather*; Convivial: *Jump into a Pleated Shirt*; Geological: "In schist, and schistose rocks are writ the bans"; Philosophical: *Crisscrossers*.

The publication of this second edition suggests that Hiebert has had his wish fulfilled, that he might "fit audience find, though few," those who read, as he says in his prefatory sonnet, "not to enlarge"

> But lovingly, to thumb each page anew,
> And chuckle at the doodles on the marge.

The implicit comparison with Milton is seriously intended: it reminds us of the loving disrespect with which Hiebert treats our poets and poetic tradition, and it encourages us, though we may lament that we have no Canadian Milton, to rejoice that we have not only Haliburton and Leacock but Hiebert. But "to thumb ... and chuckle" is better than "to rejoice." So let us take a first look or another look, as the case may be, at the doodles on the marge and follow Sarah's course, which ran like Virgil's from eclogue ("Tityre, tu . . .") to epic, from "Oh calf . . ." to these "four lines from an old Mission Song—not even her own," with which she brings *The Magma* to a faltering close :

> Now is the last spike driven,
> Now is the last tie riven,
> Now is the last speech given—
> Let's all go home !

LLOYD WHEELER

The University of Manitoba,
Winnipeg, Manitoba

Author's Introduction

SARAH BINKS, the Sweet Songstress of Saskatchewan, as she is often called, no longer needs any introduction to her ever growing list of admirers. In fact, it may be asked why another book should be added to the already voluminous and continually growing literature which deals with the work of this great Canadian. We already know about her life—we know about her tragic death. We know about her early struggles for recognition and her rise to fame. We know about the honours that were showered upon her, culminating finally in that highest award in the bestowal of the Saskatchewan people, the Wheat Pool Medal. But what is not known, or at least what is so often overlooked, is that quite apart from the Saskatchewan for which Sarah speaks, she was pre-eminently a poetess in her own right, that in a life so poor in incident and surrounded on all sides by the pastoral simplicity, if not actual severity, of the Municipality of Willows, she developed a character so rich and a personality so winsome and diverse. There is, too, a profound personal philosophy which speaks to us quite apart from the sweep and beauty of the prairies with which she is associated. It is this theme which the Author has developed. It definitely strikes a new note.

From Shakespeare's "England, my England," to a Saskatchewan wheat farm may seem to be a far cry. But that same patriotism, that same confidence and joy in his native land which is the heritage of all poets, is also Sarah's. And when she cries out in a sudden awareness of her own gumbo stretch, "The Farmer is King!" or when she sings in full throat *The Song of the Chore*, or hymns the joy of *Spreading Time*, or discusses with deep understanding but with impersonal detachment as in *To My Father, Jacob Binks*, the fine economic adjustment between the farmer and the cut-worm, we know that she speaks for the Canadian West in the language of all poets at all times. It is this which has given her the high place in the world of literature and in the hearts of her countrymen.

But there is much more to Sarah Binks than being the Laureate of Saskatchewan. Sarah was not only the expression of her day and age, she was also the product of her immediate environment. She was the product of her friends, of her books, and of the little incidents which shaped her life. She was the product of the Grade School, of her neighbours, of Mathilda Schwantzhacker, of Ole the hired man, of her grandfather the philosophical herbalist, of William Greenglow who taught her Geology, of Henry Welkin who took her to Regina. From all of these Sarah emerges as a character, as a personality, and above all, as a woman.

It has been no light task to gather together the many threads of personal and literary influence and to reconstruct from them, as in fine needlepoint, a truer, more intimate picture of Sarah Binks than we have hitherto known. Sarah, on the larger canvas, as a national figure, loses nothing thereby. But for those who like to look beyond the poetry to the poetess, for those who would see beyond the high achievement the unfolding and blossoming of the poetic spirit, this new life of Sarah Binks has been written.

There is an age in Western Canada which is fast disappearing before our very eyes; an age which began with the turn of the century and lasted at its best about thirty years. Sarah's dates, 1906 to 1929, practically define it. They were the halcyon days of Western Canada, the golden days of the dirt farmer. It was an age sandwiched between the romantic West of the "cow country" and the West of drought and relief and economic experiment. It was a prosperous age for Saskatchewan, and such periods of prosperity and commercial expansion are always accompanied by literary and artistic blossoming. On a small scale the Golden Age of Pericles in Greece, or the Elizabethan age of England, finds its counterpart in Canada's fairest and flattest province. Already in brief historical perspective that age is beginning to take on an aura of romance. Sarah Binks was its artistic expression.

Those most productive years of Sarah's also mark the high-water mark of Saskatchewan's prosperity. The price of wheat rose to fabulous heights; clean eggs, not over three days old, sold in the general stores at prices ranging all the way from twenty to twenty-six cents a dozen, whilst at the Willows and Quagmire elevators the classifications of both screenings and Durum, No. 4, Smutty, were raised to No. 3, Smutty. Liver also showed signs of a rise.

To the west the frontier had been rolled back; the tumbleweed had yielded to the sow thistle, the coyote had vanished from the plains, and with the disappearance of these great herds, his last source of Vitamin B gone, disappeared also the prairie Indian, a proud and picturesque figure in overalls and plug hat—swept away before the ruthless march of civilization. The land was open for wheat. No economic cloud marked the Saskatchewan horizon; mortgage money could be had at any time for twelve per cent, and the dry belt, which years later was to creep north and eastward over a country already desiccated by prohibition laws, still lay in the heart of the Great American Desert.

It is claimed by some writers that Sarah Binks sprang spontaneously from Saskatchewan's alkaline soil, that she was an isolated genius such as the ages have produced from time to time with no significance beyond her unparalleled talent. With this view the Author takes exception. Sarah Binks was the product of her soil and her roots go deep. But more than that, she was an expression of her environment and her age. Without Saskatchewan at its greatest, at its golden age, Sarah would have been just another poetess. Sarah was the daughter and the granddaughter of a dirt farmer; she loved the soil and much of Jacob Binks's passion for another quarter section flowed in her veins. Her love for the paternal acres was a real love, she believed in the rotation of crops and, in the fall, after the ploughing was done, she spread the fertilizer with a lavish hand. "The farmer is king!" she cries,

> The farmer is king of his packer and plough,
> Of his harrows and binders and breakers,
> He is lord of the pig, and Czar of the cow
> On his hundred and sixty-odd acres.

> The farmer is monarch in high estate,
> Of his barn and his backhouse and byre,
> And all the buildings behind the gate
> Of his two-odd miles of barbed wire.
>
> The farmer is even Caesar of freight
> And tariff and tax, comes election,
> And from then until then he can abdicate,
> And be king on his own quarter section.
>
> The farmer is king, oh, the farmer is king,
> And except for his wife and his daughter,
> Who boss him around, he runs the thing,
> Come drought, come hell or high water.

It is significant, too, that Sarah Binks should have seized upon Warden and Rockbuster's *First Steps in Geology* and made it so singularly her own. Geology to her was the farm extended to the outer world, to the larger life. Any other book at that period of her life would have left her cold. It is undoubtedly true, to quote Principal Pinhole, "If the benign fates which rule the lives of men had passed William Greenglow in Geology II and had given him a supplemental in Maths II instead, Sarah's songs would not have been touched to the same extent. The binomial theorem as I understand it is by no means the same as the theory of crustal movements, and it is just because the one deals with rocks and the other has to do with figures without rocks, that the whole Neo-Geo-Literary school of literature is different by just that much. In fact some other province might have got the credit."

Sarah Binks has raised her home province of Saskatchewan to its highest prairie level. Unschooled, but unspoiled, this simple country girl has captured in her net of poesy the flatness of that great province. Like a sylph she wanders through its bluffs and coulees, across its haylands, its alkali flats, its gumbo stretches, its gopher meadows:

> Hark! Like a mellow fiddle moaning,
> Through the reed-grass sighing,
> Through a gnarled branch groaning,
> Comes the Poet—
> Sylph-like,

Gaunt-like,
Poeming—
And his eyes are stars,
And his mouth is foaming.

Thus, Sarah herself, in the divine frenzy. No wonder she is called the Sweet Songstress of Saskatchewan. Indeed she could be called much more. No other poet has so expressed the Saskatchewan soul. No other poet has caught in deathless lines so much of its elusive spirit, the baldness of its prairies, the alkalinity of its soil, the richness of its insect life.

In presenting this new study of the life and works of the Sweet Songstress the Author feels that he is filling a long-felt want. Much has already been written, much more remains to be written, but hitherto no such complete study of the life and character of Sarah Binks has been published. The papers which have appeared from time to time have been fragmentary, generally critical studies dealing with one phase of her life or with a group of poems. Special mention must be made of the numerous papers of Horace P. Marrowfat, B.A., Professor Emeritus of English and Swimming, of St Midget's College; of Dr Taj Mahal, D.O., of British Columbia; and of the Proceedings of the Ladies' Literary League of Quagmire. These papers and publications have been of especial value in the preparation of this book, and proper acknowledgements have been made wherever it was considered absolutely necessary.

The Author also wishes to express his indebtedness to the recent work, *Great Lives and Great Loves*, by Miss Rosalind Drool, and to the publishers, Bunnybooks Ltd., for permission to quote therefrom. Miss Drool's intense and even introspective searchings into certain phases of Sarah Binks's life have been of great interest, more especially since her own personal offer to pursue further studies "at considerable lengths" has also heightened an interest in Miss Drool.

The great source of material for the student of Sarah Binks is, of course, the Binksian Collection in the Provincial Archives of Saskatchewan. This, together with the letters of Mathilda, has been the supply upon which all other students have hitherto drawn. But much inference has been published as fact. Many of the details of Sarah's life are still vague and have still to be filled in. There is, however, a great wealth of material still unturned and unexploited around Willows, Sarah's birthplace. The Author has not hesitated to make use of this material where it could be published.

It has been the aim of the Author at all times to give a deeper, truer meaning to the poetic heritage which belongs to Sarah, the unspoiled child of the soil. Sarah's lyrical poetry, small as it is in bulk, ranks among the rarest treasures of Canadian literature. The poems which have been included in this work are most of them well known, but no apology need be made for their repetition. Quite apart from their intrinsic beauty, they are significant in that they are expressions of facts and events in her life. Sarah, more than most poets, seizes upon the trivial, or what to less souls would appear trivial, incident and experience, for example the loss of Ole's ear by a duck, as an occasion for a lyrical outburst of pulsating beauty. These poems can only be understood within the context of Sarah's life, and free use has therefore been made of them. No one has ever wanted to copyright any of Sarah's poems, and they have therefore been quoted at length—wholly, partly, or just simply quoted.

In addition to the field work done in and around Willows the Author has made a special journey to Quorum, Saskatchewan, at which place Mrs Steve Grizzlykick (Mathilda) was interviewed, and to Vertigo, Manitoba, where Mrs Pete Cattalo was questioned concerning Ole. Although the actual field data obtained in these investigations cannot be published, they have been of much value in giving atmosphere and in interpreting the scene around Willows and Quagmire during and immediately preceding the time when Sarah wrote *Wash Out on the Line*.

The Author is greatly indebted to the Editor of *The Horsebreeder's Gazette* for the opportunity of going through his files, and also, when he was out to lunch, his desk. Much interesting information was available here.

In the case of the Editor of *Swine and Kine* no files had been kept, but permission was given to interview the secretary and later on to take her out to the local dance. The information here was exceptionally good.

The Author in particular wishes to express his indebtedness to the Quagmire Malting and Brewing Company for

much of the material embodied in this book, and to the
Dominion Distillers, Limited, who so kindly read the proofs.

PAUL HIEBERT
The Burrs
Carman, Manitoba
1946

Contents

I

Childhood and Early Life

A PLAIN SHAFT of composition stone with the simple inscription:

HERE LIES
SARAH BINKS

marks the last resting place of the Sweet Songstress of Saskatchewan. Below the inscription at the base of the shaft in smaller letters is carved the motto: ALONE, and above it in larger type:

THIS MONUMENT WAS ERECTED BY THE
CITIZENS OF THE MUNICIPALITY
OF NORTH WILLOWS
AND WAS UNVEILED ON JULY 1, 1931
BY
THE HON. AUGUSTUS E. WINDHEAVER
IN THE PRESENCE OF
THE REEVE AND COUNCIL

Here follow the names of the reeve and councillors together with the names of a number of outstanding statesmen of the day. Truly a fitting tribute to so great a woman. And it is no less a tribute to the Province of Saskatchewan that on the occasion of the unveiling of this monument the register of names at the Commercial House at Willows should be at the same time the roster of the greatest of Saskatchewan's sons. The Hon. A. E. Windheaver writes of that occasion in a letter [1] to his committee:

---

[1] Private letter, now in possession of the Author.

It was hot as hell! There was no making it by road and we could have arranged for a hot box to hold the 4:46 for half an hour, but it was no use. We had to stick it until everybody was through. I think I was wise to leave out the tariff in my speech. This Sarah seems to be something of a tin god around here.

Something of a god! The tribute of a great statesman to a great artist and a great woman.

Halfway between Oak Bluff and Quagmire in Saskatchewan lies the little town of North Willows. Its public buildings are unpretentious but pure in architectural style. A post office, two general stores, Charley Wong's restaurant and billiard parlour, two United churches, the Commercial House (Lib.), the Clarendon Hotel (Cons.), a drug store, a consolidated school, and eighteen filling stations, make up the east side of Railway Avenue, its chief commercial street. On the west side Railway Avenue is taken up by the depot, the lumber yard and four elevators. At right angles to Railway Avenue runs Post Office Street, so called because the post office was on this street before the last provincial election. It is, however, generally known simply as the Correction Line.

Business in Willows is not what it used to be. The Board of Trade meets every Thursday night above Charley Wong's, and the younger set of the town is beginning to give up auction bridge in favour of contract, but in spite of these signs of progress there has been little real growth for several years. The town is now in what is known as the dry belt. Once it boasted seven elevators; one was torn down and two were destroyed by fire and have not been rebuilt. But Willows has little need for commercial greatness. It lives in its glorious past, and to its shrine every year come hundreds who pause for a brief moment at the Clarendon Hotel or the Commercial House, or buy gasoline at the "Sarah Filling Station."

If we follow Post Office Street, or the Correction Line, due east for half a mile to where it corrects we come to Willow View Cemetery where Sarah Binks's monument stands. From a distance it appears to rise in lonely grandeur. If we follow Post Office Street due west for a mile and a quarter from the town, we come to the North East Quarter of Section 37, Township 21, Range 9, West, the former home of Sarah Binks herself. Little remains of the old homestead. The house itself has been torn down by souvenir hunters, one of the barns leans drunkenly and the other is about to fall. Gophers play on the site of the little corral where Sarah kept the calf, wild roses grow where once were beans and potatoes. In the coulee, now dry, that ran behind the house, a meadowlark has built its nest. It may have been that Sarah, with the prophetic eye of the poetess, visualized this scene when, in her later years, she wrote those famous lines, now inscribed in bronze over the gateway of St Midget's, entitled *Ode to a Deserted Farm*:

> How changed and bleak the meadows lie
> And overgrown with hay,
> The fields of oats and barley
> Where the binder twined its way!
>
> With doors ajar the cottage stands
> Deserted on the hill—
> No welcome bark, no thudding hoof,
> And the voice of the pig is still.

The west was still the West in the days when Jacob and Agathea Binks first homesteaded the N. E. ¼ Sec. 37, Township 21, R. 9, W. To the east lay Oak Bluff, the end of the steel. To the west stretched the boundless prairies of the North West Territories, in which, to quote Sarah's own words, "The hand of man hath never trod." Here was the home of the coyote and the gopher, the antelope still flaunted his lack of tail to the western wind, and the pensive mosquito wandered unafraid. A region rich in historical interests and traditions, of tales of Indian fights with their squaws, of squaws with the Mounted Police. Willows was then Wallows, and the very name, Oak Bluff, was derived from an old Indian word, or combination of words, indicating that at that spot the white man had been frightened or, to use the Indian term, "bluffed" at a conference between Chief Buffalo Chip and Colonel MacSqueamish, the outcome being described by the chief in the Cree dialect as being "oke," meaning very good, or excellent.

Into this free and untrammelled country came Jacob Binks and his wife Agathea (née Agathea Thurnow), the parents of Sarah. It is not known exactly from where they came but, from a report of a conversation in front of the post office, and from the fact that Sarah was often wont to refer to herself proudly as a daughter of the Old South, it is now generally accepted that they came from South Dakota. Beyond this fact we know little of the Binks antecedents. The Thurnows, however, are said to have traced their family back to Confederation. The parish records in Quoddykodiac in New Brunswick show that a daughter Agathea was born to one Abram Turnip and that the Turnips later moved to South Dakota. The name Turnip may have been Americanized to Thurnip and later to Thurnow.

Prosperity smiled upon Jacob and Agathea Binks. The original sod house of the homesteader was replaced by a more pretentious frame building faced with best quality tarpaper and having an outside stairs leading to the guest room over the kitchen roof. One entered the "lean-to" or antechamber before reaching the main body of the house and living quarters. This antechamber served the purpose of receiving and storage room. In it was kept the fuel, the churn, the harnesses undergoing repair, here the chickens were plucked, the eggs collected, and here slept Rover, the dog, and Ole, the hired man. Through the antechamber one passed into the kitchen and from there into the parlour which in turn led into the bedrooms.

The birthplace of Sarah has been described as having been furnished with some taste. Around the walls of the parlour were hung in pairs the ancestral portraits; Jacob and Agathea Binks in bevelled glass and gilt frames occupied the south wall. A crayon enlargement of Grandfather Thadeus T. Thurnow, together with a black-and-white steel engraving of a prize sheep which bore a remarkable resemblance to the old gentleman, occupied the north wall. The gaze of all four was thoughtfully concentrated upon the Quebec heater which stood in the mathematical centre of the room. This heater, when glowing with fire, not only served the purpose of heating the room, but acted during the night as a species of navigating light from the bedrooms to the outdoors via the kitchen when the occasion required. The keynote of severely artistic, almost geometrical simplicity, marked the arrangement of the three chairs and sideboard which completed the appointments.

The parlour was used only on great occasions. Rover and Ole were never allowed to use this room if we except the one occasion when, according to Dr Taj Mahal, who claims to have examined the floor, the former made a complete circuit of the freshly painted surface, paused for a moment at one of the chairs and departed through the north window.

The kitchen, too, was not without its artistic touches, but here a lighter and more imaginative motif prevails, the influence of the Thurnows to which Sarah's artistic and imaginative qualities may always be referred. Two calendars in particular mark the aesthetic discrimination of the home. One shows a vessel in full sail in dangerous proximity to the Eddystone Light, and the other, of more idyllic theme, shows in an orchard a young woman of beautiful proportions offering a cherry to a young man of her acquaintance. One of these calendars is said by experts to be an original. (Both are preserved in the Binksian collection.) But quite apart from the cultural influence which these two great pictures must have had upon the susceptible mind of the young Sarah, they bear a great significance in that they enable us to fix with considerable certainty the dates of several of her early poems. Professor R. Ambush has called attention to the fact that the date of April 1st bears the entry "caff," and that this refers to the date on which Sarah's pet calf was born and that those poignant lines of *Calf* could not have been written before this date and were probably written soon after since it had not yet received a name:

> Oh calf, that gambolled by my door,
> Who made me rich who now am poor,
> That licked my hand with milk bespread,
> Oh calf, calf! Art dead, art dead?

> Oh calf, I sit and languish, calf,
> With sombre face, I cannot laugh,
> Can I forget thy playful bunts?
> Oh calf, calf, that loved me once!

> With mildewed optics, deathlike, still,
> My nights are damp, my days are chill,
> I weep again with doleful sniff,
> Oh, calf, calf, so dead, so stiff.

Sarah was the second or possibly the third child of Agathea and Jacob Binks. None of the other children survived their infancy, and Agathea Binks either died or abdicated while Sarah was still a child. But there is no evidence that Sarah was lonesome. She seems to have loved solitude and although some of her later work, notably that of her early Post Regina period, displays a touch of the morbid whose origin psychologists could undoubtedly trace to her childhood, there seems to be no doubt that her early girlhood was spent like that of other children of her day. She was a happy and a healthy child. She assisted in the simple household chores of weeding the garden, gathering the eggs, and picking the potato bugs.[1] During the summer months the little Sarah, her lunch pail under her arm, trudged the mile and a quarter to the one-roomed school at Willows. Her education was sporadic at best. More often than not, especially as she grew older, she was obliged to stay at home and help around the farm. Moreover Jacob Binks was opposed to much education. "There ain't no dam' sense in all this book-learning" was the frequent expression of his inner conviction and his public policy, as a result of which he was elected and invariably re-elected to the School Board.

But if Sarah's formal education was neglected, if her acquaintance with the great authors was a mere nodding acquaintance, she learned all the more from the big school of nature. Nature to her was something alive, and the life of the farm, wild as well as domestic, acquired in her eyes a character and a personality. The lowly blade of grass and the stately horse were equally objects of her sympathetic speculations. She understood the grasshoppers and held them in contempt, whereas the gophers, whose inclusion in the

---

[1] Miss Iguana Binks-Barkingwell, of St Olafs-Down-the-Drain, Hants, Hurts, Harts, England, who claims to be a distant kinswoman of Sarah Binks, has recently made a presentation to the Saskatchewan Zoological Society of a mounted collection of potato bugs from all parts of the Empire, to be known as the Binksian Collection. Dr Termite of Toronto has raised the question, and with it a storm of controversy, as to whether the so-called "young potato bugs" in this collection are not actually lady-bugs. It is unfortunate, in the Author's opinion, that this controversy should have arisen over a collection of potato bugs which was originally conceived to do honour to a great poetess.

primordial curse had, according to Jacob Binks, been omitted only through some oversight on the part of the Creator, were to Sarah a constant source of humorous amusement. For the perennial calf she had a womanly affection, and its stupidity enthralled her. She was keenly aware of the beauty of sky and field. She loved the hot sunlight of the afternoon and the feel of the wind on her cheek. One need only read *My Garden* and *The Bug* to realize how deep is Sarah's sympathetic understanding of nature.

MY GARDEN

A little blade of grass I see,
Its banner waving wild and free,
And I wonder if in time to come
'Twill be a great big onion;
We cannot tell, we do not know,
For oft we reap and didn't sow;
We plant the hairy coconut,
With hope serene and sturdy—but
We cannot tell, for who can say,
We plant the oats and reap the hay,
We sow the apple, reap the worm,
We tread the worm and reap the turn:
Too much, too much for us this thought,
With much too much exertion fraught;
In faith we get the garden dug—
And what do we reap—we reap the bug,
In goodly faith we plant the seed,
Tomorrow morn we reap the weed.

THE BUG

In a little nook, a nooklet,
There beside a babbling brooklet,
Sits a little bug, a beetle,
Browsing in a little volume,
Reading in a brand new booklet,
Studying the spinal column,
Learning where to put his needle,
Get me with his little hooklet.

But not only is Sarah's understanding of nature a sympathetic one but her love for the animal life is deep and abiding. One need only recall *The Goose*, or *The Apple*, or the ever popular *Song to the Cow*, songs which Bishop Puddy [1] of Bingobingoland places in the very first rank.

THE GOOSE

The goose, a noisome bird to chatter,
But handsome on a garnished platter,
A loathsome brute to toil among,
But caught and killed and cooked and hung,
Before a crackling fire,
A songster to admire.

THE APPLE

Today as I an apple mulched
A worm I fain did bite in twain,
'Twas curled up in its little world
Where it in peace had lain;
So ruthlessly did I disturb
The little worm, helpless, infirm,
Yet no remorse did shake my soul,
No pricks of conscience make me squirm.

SONG TO THE COW

I'll take no cow that fails to sing,
Or throstle with its horn,
Her milk must stimulate like tea,
Her tail stretch to infinity,
And her nose be plush-like and warm
Amorous of optic, mild but quick
To perceive where the grass is pale,
A rhomboid snout, a mellow lick,
And a breath like ale—
These attributes in a cow, I deem,
Are the best to be had and win my esteem.

---

[1] Rev. Beckus Puddy, *A Comparative Study of the Literature of Saskatchewan with that of Easter Island. The Sunday Sleep,* Vol. 1, No. 1. (Out of Print.)

" 'Amorous of optic . . . breath like ale!' What imagery! It is in lines like these," says Miss Rosalind Drool, "with their haunting cadence that Miss Binks expresses the great soul of Saskatchewan. One wonders how she does it."

2

Ole

ONE MAY TRACE many influences which affected Sarah's work, influences great and small which touched her here and there; Ole, Rover, William Greenglow, Henry Welkin, Grandfather Thurnow, strong, masculine influences which affected her outlook, touching her mind, and leaving their light and sometimes their shadow upon her poetry. But to Ole, cheerful hard-working Ole, big of heart and feet, must go the honour of having been the first to put the young Sarah upon the path of poesy. It is significant, even symbolical, that just as years ago on the morning after Dominion Day, Ole himself was traced for miles across the alkali flats that lie north of Willows, so today one traces his splendid footprints across the dazzling pages of Saskatchewan literature.

Ole's other name is not known, or if it ever was known it has been forgotten. He answered simply to the name of Ole. When, on the rare occasions a more formal address became necessary as when the extra mail-order catalogue arrived, it became, Ole, c/o J. Binks. Professor Ambush has suggested that the name Ole may be a diminutive of Olafur or perhaps of Oleander, but no diminutive can possibly apply. He was above all a big man such as the West is fond of producing. His feet found their way with difficulty through the trousers of his store suit, his shoulders were of gnarled oak, and his two hands swung at his sides like slabs of teak. He was noted for his great strength. He could haul the stoneboat with its two full water barrels from the coulee to the house, and when, as sometimes happened, a horse would straddle the barbed wire fence, he would assist it from its predicament by lifting one end or another as the circumstances required. He had an equine playfulness and would toss Mathilda, even

when eighteen and already large for her age, from the ground
to the hayloft with great ease and to her infinite delight.

But if Ole's strength was great, his good nature and cheer-
fulness were even greater. No one is known ever to have
offended Ole. His mind had that simplicity and directness and
that acceptance of the world which one associates with his
race and occupation. He and Rover were inseparable; Ole
shared his lunches in the field with Rover, and the latter
shared his fleas at night with Ole. Both had a deep and abiding
affection for Sarah.

Neither Rover nor Ole actually wrote any poetry, at
least none has come down to us unless we accept the terse
verses, often fragmentary and sometimes illustrated, which
Ole was fond of writing upon the granaries and other small
buildings with a piece of coal. (Two of these boards, one of
doubtful authenticity, are known to exist in private collections of Binksiana.) But where both Ole's and Rover's chief
influence upon Sarah's poetic talent lay, was that it was they
who first taught her the singing quality of verse. Rover's
voice had a deep and throbbing cadence with which he
tended to experiment in metrical forms especially on moonlight nights. Grandfather Thurnow's remark, that "At least
he cuts it up into stove lengths," was at once a recognition
of Rover's success and an appreciation of his talent. Ole's
voice, on the other hand, was a high falsetto and tended to
break. When it broke it took on a certain screeching quality,
not altogether pleasant in itself, but particularly well adapted
to the old Norse ballads and folksongs which he rendered
with full pedal and with an abandon which aroused Sarah's
boundless admiration. He translated these songs freely—almost too freely. But he planted the seeds of poesy in Sarah's
heart, nor could Jacob Binks's frequent admonition to "Shut
up, you dam' squarehead!" prevent the seeds from sprouting.

Between Ole and Sarah there was a bond which was never
broken. She leaned heavily on him throughout her life, both
in the matter of chores and in the matter of inspiration; "My
staff and my stick, my Pole and my prop," she says of him
in a fragment of verse in which she reveals a rather hazy
conception of the geography of northern Europe but acknowledges her debt. Ole was her slave and her dependable friend.
It was he who first taught her the satisfaction of the occasional pipe, he taught her to swim in the dugout, he taught

her all he knew about handling a calf, about farm machinery, and about Mathilda.

For Sarah, poetry was ever the expression of the soul, whether it was her own soul or somebody else's or simply that of Saskatchewan. In *The Hired Man on Saturday Night* she expresses Ole's soul and in its moment of greatest elation.

THE HIRED MAN ON SATURDAY NIGHT

A horse! A horse! Give me a horse,
To dash across the frozen north,
And wallow in the mire,
A noble barb with cloven hoof,
With brazen wings and blatant snoof,
And molten eyes of fire.

I'll carve a furlong through the snow,
And bring the bastard she-cat low,
And bind her to a tree,
That ding-bat dire, shall put her sire,
Out of the frying pan into the fire,
Where e'er she be.

With gathered rage of many an age,
I'll blot the boar from off the page,
And twist his face;
I'll smite the rooster in the snow,
And crafty Rover, dumb with woe,
Shall curse his race.

I'll tie a reef knot in the tail
Of Barney's bull—with tooth and nail
I'll fill his day with gloom;
The calf shall wail, the cow shall quail,
The horse shall totter and grow pale—
Give me room!

It would appear that on Ole's one free evening of the week he developed a sense of aloofness from farm animals which excluded even Rover. The poem does not approximate the high standard which Sarah usually sets for herself. However it has a swing and rhythm and Professor Marrowfat rates it very highly. He says, "Sarah has hit it on the nose. I don't know much about farm animals, my line being literature. But I know just the feeling that Ole has. I have it myself almost every Saturday night." Nevertheless, in the opinion of the Author, Sarah expresses the feeling more accurately in *Steeds*. Here the sense of elation is combined with the rush and sweep of horses. The occasion of this poem was the time when Ole returned from Willows on the late afternoon of election day, 1911. On that occasion he is alleged to have disappeared with two demijohns of linseed oil which he was transporting with his team from the Liberal to the Conservative Committee rooms. (The incident is recalled in the memoirs of the Hon. Grafton Tabernackel, at that time Administrator of the Farm Implement Oiling and Greasing Act.)

STEEDS

I have two dashing, prancing steeds,
Buttercup and Dairy Queen,
What for spirit, what for speed,
Matches this amazing team?
One is roan and one is plaid,
One a mare, and one a lad,
One a pacer, one a trotter,
One a son, and one a daughter:
When they're fastened side by side,
Yoked together in the traces,
Joyfully prepare to ride
O'er the big and open spaces;
Whoopee! Swift across the stubble,
Over boulders, banks and rubble,
Up the hill and down the glen,
Cross the county—back again,
Through the fence and greenhouse go,
Pumpkin garden—to and fro,
Pounding, puffing, like a dragon,
Kill the calf and smash the wagon,
Through the hayloft, dust and smother,
In one end and out the other—
Zowie! When their spirit's up!
Dairy Queen and Buttercup!

On an even higher level is the short poem, *The Cursed Duck*, a poem in which Sarah reveals her sympathetic nature and essential womanhood following the loss of one of Ole's ears one Sunday morning. The ducks on the Binks' farm had a passion for vegetables to which Sarah's garden bore mute testimony every fall, and it is supposed that Ole had inadvertently fallen asleep in or near the vegetable patch.

THE CURSED DUCK

A cursed duck pecked off his ear,
And his face grew peaked and pale;
"Oh, how can a woman love me now?"
Was his constant and lonely wail;
But a woman came, and she loved the man,
With a love serene and clear—
She loved him as only a woman can love
A man with only one ear.

It is undoubtedly to Ole's influence that we owe the *Song of the Sea*, characterized by Professor Dumplin [1] as ". . . the finest sea song ever to come out of the dry belt." Sarah had never seen the sea, in fact it was not until years later that she saw Lake Wascana, but the blood of the Vikings flowed in Ole's veins, and from Ole's veins to Sarah's verse was but a step:

SONG OF THE SEA

All hail, all hail, to the shriek of the gale,
Huzzah, huzzah, to the boat,
    As with mainsail rent,
    And the keel all bent,
    The mainfore gallant sail split like a tent,
    The captain dead,
    And the mate in bed,
The ship's carpenter downstairs sounding the lead,
She runs amuck, and she runs amoke,
O'er the rollicking, frolicking, bounding main.

[1] Bootlick and Dumplin, *Some Observations on the Marine Life of the South Saskatchewan River and Its Beaches*. Trans. Proc. Lit. Phil. Sci. Soc. Agric. Sask. (7) 11, 1937.

Rear Admiral R. N. Saltspit, retired, in a letter to the *Times* calls attention to a technical error in this poem in that the duties of the ship's carpenter are not to sound the lead but to swing it, but he adds in commendation, "The colonies are doing some remarkable things. Miss Binks charts her way through the shoals and intricacies of metre in a way that makes us all feel four sheets in the wind. Our Laureate may have to look to his laurels."

Sarah's greatest poem to Ole is undoubtedly *Where Shall I Find*. As in so many other of her greatest lines the spirit of the West breathes through and through it. Here she not only extols Ole's virtues as a man, but also pays splendid tribute to that manhood in a hired capacity.

WHERE SHALL I FIND

Where shall I find a hired man
For homely destiny to toil,
To mend harnesses,
And shovel cement,
And boil oil.

Where shall I find a hired man,
To gather rocks and do the chores,
To harrow wide,
And plough deep,
The big outdoors.

Where shall I find a hired man
With a single passion for his job,
With thoughts of work,
And nothing else,
Within his knob.

Where shall I search for a hired man,
With corded arms and knotted knees,
With beamed shoulders,
And feet
Like Hercules'.

At a recent joint meeting of The Ladies' Literary League of Quagmire, and The Former Friends of Ole, Willows Chapter, it was decided to have this poem carved upon Ole's tombstone when he returns from Bear Lake, if ever. In rising to propose a raffle to defray the expenses of this monument, Mrs Pete Cattalo, F.F.O., paid a tribute to Ole as well as to Sarah when she said, "It is a big poem. It's going to cost us money to have this done. But then Ole was a big man, big in every way, you can take it from me."

3

Mathilda

IT IS A singular fact that all the influences in Sarah's life were masculine with the exception of Mathilda. Even here, one can hardly say that Mathilda, in spite of her close friendship and years of association, was actually an influence in Sarah's work; one might say that she served as a foil and as an occasion for Sarah's poems rather than as an actual source of inspiration. Nevertheless, to Mathilda the great world of literature must acknowledge an unrepayable debt. Without her the Grizzlykick Symphony of poems would never have been written. Through her our knowledge and understanding of Sarah's character and personality have been extended. But above all, it is through her collection of Sarah's letters, carefully preserved, that we are able to piece together the often sketchy outline of Sarah's life. Mathilda was always a Sarah worshipper; moreover she had that priceless gift of acquisitiveness which marks the true collector. When she was finally induced to sell her collection to the Binksian Society it included not only the priceless letters but also various items of her own personal interest such as valentines, comic post cards, newspaper clippings of advertisements for long eyelashes and the improvement of the "figure," and a relic, which from the colour and texture was long believed to be a lock of Ole's hair but which since has been shown to be a gopher tail.[1] Mathilda valued this collection highly, and only her approaching marriage induced her to part with it. "If I hadent had to get married I wouldent take a cent lessen twenty five dollars for them," she writes to the Secretary of

---

[1] The complete collection, with the exception of the comic post cards, is preserved in the Binksian Collection.

the Binksian Society during the course of the protracted negotiations which finally led to this collection being acquired for the Nation.

Mathilda Schwantzhacker was the thirteenth daughter of Kurt Schwantzhacker who occupied the South East Quarter of Section 37, Township 21, Range 9, West. The Schwantzhackers and the Binks were therefore neighbours a half mile apart, and lived in reasonable amity except on those occasions when the horses strayed through the barbed wire or when Ole and Rover practised their duets. Kurt Schwantzhacker was a dirt farmer of the better class, independent to the point of obstinacy. His farm supported him in all things even to the extent of a species of wild rhubarb of which he harvested a small crop every year in the belief that it was tobacco. He believed in being self-sustaining and raised his own food, his clothing, and his help with the somewhat indifferent cooperation of his wife. The belief that the farm could satisfy every need was not shared, however, by the thirteen Schwantzhacker girls, and they accordingly welcomed Ole as an honoured guest. They paid frequent calls on Sarah, and when the thirteen Schwantzhacker sisters came calling on Sunday afternoon, carefully picking their way in single file across the pasture which separated the two farms, the resemblance to an ancient Druid procession was very close. Ole was always moved by this fine sight; some latent memory of his Viking ancestry must have stirred in his blood, but to Sarah the only really welcome visitor among the thirteen was Mathilda. She was by far the best looking of the thirteen, certainly she was the least cross-eyed; she was Sarah's own age, she had been her confidante at school, and above all she was the only one who showed any interest in and appreciation for poetry.

It was Mathilda who first introduced Sarah to German literature. Literature in any language did not occupy a particularly high place in the Schwantzhacker culture, but the sisters, although they spoke German, as they were anxious to have it understood, "only in the home," nevertheless still sang some of the folksongs of their parents' homeland, generally in chorus, and often, it is said, to drown out Rover and Ole. Sarah knew no German but Mathilda taught her some of the songs, the words and melodies at least, without much regard for their meaning. But Sarah's mind was always

awake to any poetic opportunity. She borrowed Kurt
Schwantzhacker's dictionary and translated. Several of these
translations have come down to us, but they have generally
been omitted from the anthologies of Sarah's works as not
being truly representative of Sarah and Saskatchewan, and
may, in fact, represent the combined efforts of Sarah and
Mathilda. Her best known, and undoubtedly finest of these
translations, are those of Heine's *Du Bist Wie Eine Blume*,
and *Die Lorelei*. The former is an almost perfect translation,
but in the case of the *Lorelie* Sarah makes the easily under-
standable mistake of translating "Lorelei" as "laurel's egg"
instead of "Laura's Eye."

DU BIST WIE EINE BLUME (*Transl.*)

You are like one flower,
So swell, so good, and clean,
I look you on and longing,
Slinks me the heart between :

Me is as if the hands I
On head yours put them should,
Praying that God you preserve,
So swell, so clean, and good.

THE LAUREL'S EGG (*Die Lorelei*)

I know not what shall it betoken,
    That I so sorrowful seem,
A marklet from out of old, spoken,
    That comes me not out of the bean.

The loft is cool and it darkles,
    And ruefully floweth the Clean,
The top of the mountain-top sparkles,
    In evening sun-shine sheen.

The fairest young woman sitteth,
    There wonderful up on top,
Her golden-like outfit glitteth,
    She combeth her golden mop;

> She combs it with golden comb-full
> And sings one song thereto,
> That has one wonderful, wonderful,
> And powerful toodle-di-doo.
>
> The shipper in very small shiplet,
> Begrabs it with very wild cry,
> He looks not the rock and the riplet,
> He looks but up top on the high.
>
> I believe that the whales will devour,
> The end of the shipper and ship,
> And that has in her singing bower,
> The Laurel's egg done it.

Sarah's translation of the river Rhein as the river "Clean" is masterful. But it must be confessed, even among her most ardent admirers, that she is not at her best in a translation. She tends to be too literal, and in her efforts to preserve form and rhyme she loses, if not the actual content, at least some of the spirit of the original. Von Knödel,[1] in his study of these translations, asserts that in her rendering of *Mit den Pfeil und Bogen*, etc. as

> With the file, and bending,
> Come the gripes a-rending,

she has lost not only the spirit but the form and content as well, but admits that she has improved on the original, for which, with a narrow nationalism, he is inclined to give Mathilda the credit.

Sarah is certainly not at her best in translation, at least not from the German. What she might have done with translations from the Portugese or the Greek, or the Hindustanee, as Professor Marrowfat suggests, we cannot say. Such statements as Marrowfat's "Had Mathilda and her twelve sisters been Swahili girls such as I have seen in Africa, we might have another story to tell," belong to the field of idle specu-

---

[1] Von Knödel, *Geographic and Dietetic Influences upon Nordic Culture as Revealed in the Works of the Canadian Poetess. Mathilda Schwantzhacker.* Doctor's Thesis, University of Klein-furth.

lation and not to literary criticism; certainly Professor
Marrowfat's ethnological studies cannot be applied to comparative literature.

It may be that we dismiss Sarah's translations too lightly.
Time and a more intensive study may reveal treasures that
are still hidden to this generation. All we can say at present
is that they do not express the Saskatchewan soul. But in
dismissing them we do not detract from her peculiar genius
any more than when we say that her patriotic poems, written
during the war, were unworthy of her talents. No poet is
uniformly good, and least of all a poetess. It is the privilege
of the artist to experiment with matter and form, to find herself and her highest type of expression, and that the patriotic
poem failed to represent this highest expression of herself
Sarah was quick to discover. Not that we can ever attribute
to Sarah a narrow sectarianism or a parochial outlook, even
in such poems as *Wash Out on the Line*. There are times
when she rises to splendid heights of pure patriotism as in

> Shall Freedom shriek again, shall Freedom wail,
> Or stand at last, aghast, with unfurled tail,
> Shall it beneath the iron tyrant's gum-shoe quail?
> Nay! Not while yet is left the wind wherewith
>   to sound
> The bagpipe, not while yet is left the stick
>   wherewith to pound
> The snare-drum, not while yet the blood of
>   Christopher Columbus
> Flows in our veins, shall these our foes, succumb
>   us.

But she realizes that she cannot for long maintain the high
tempo and the martial sweep which the patriotic poem
demands. Hers was the pastoral simplicity of the plains, hers
the gentle dust storm, the dying calf, the long, somnolent
afternoon of the drought summer. Give her a field mouse, a
grasshopper, or a jam pail of potato bugs and her poetry
gushed forth unbidden, uncalled for, and unrestrained. Not
until she had studied geology did she rise to the larger outlook. Until then her patriotism was negative in character, a
denial of others, rather than an assertion of her own. For it
was Mathilda's twelve sisters who inspired most of her

patriotic verse, and the Schwantzhacker girls were kept almost as busy in destroying verses as Sarah was in writing them. She sent them over with Ole. She presented them as parting gifts to her guests on Sunday afternoons, she tied them around the necks of their ducks when they came to the Binks's coulee. At times when the wind was in the right direction she fastened them to the tumbleweed and lifted it across the barbed wire. She exhausted her vocabulary and her knowledge of the anatomy of farm animals in her search for the precise word in which to express her feelings towards the Schwantzhacker sisters.

At first glance one is inclined to regard this series of verses in the light of another of those feuds which have ever made the study of literature so fascinating. But the frequent references to the physical features of the Schwantzhacker farm as well as to those of the Schwantzacker sisters, and above all her emphasis upon their foreign extraction, definitely place this group of her poems as a patriotic effort. That this effort has not added to her fame was due to her youth. Sarah was not to acquire that wider patriotism until she had studied geology, in fact not until she had been to Regina. But what she did acquire at this stage was that easy delivery which marks the master of technique. Sarah's conceptions were always quick, and her emotional responses immediate. None of those qualities which mark the poetess at her greatest were lacking except experience. That she was already aware of her genius and at the same time conscious of her limitations she reveals in those beautiful lines, *The Genius*, a little gem of self-revelation, in which she pictures herself as already the complete artist:

THE GENIUS

I'm a genius, I'm a genius,
    What more can I desire,
I toot upon my little flute,
    And twang upon my lyre;

I dabble in oil paint,
    In cinnebar and ochre,
All night I am dissipated,
    And play poker.

In my little book, in my little book,
  I write verses,
Sometimes they don't rhyme—
  Curses!

Sarah was finding herself. That unsureness, "Sometimes
they don't rhyme, curses!" was to leave her at this stage.
It is no exaggeration to say that technically she reached her
full perfection during the poems of the patriotic period. One
need only compare *The Parson's Patch*, written in the early
fall, with *Ode to Spring*, written the following March, to
appreciate the tremendous strides she had made:

THE PARSON'S PATCH

Pathetic patch, a turnip or two,
A onion, a lettuce, a handful of maize,
A sprig of parsley, and that is all
That meets our gaze.

Here we can see with what loving care,
Poked and patted by the parson's hand,
They flourished in their meek mild way,
Just as the parson had.

And now as we turn from the parson's patch
Let us turn our eyes inwards,
And after a few minutes' contemplation,
The moral will be visible.

Here we have already the Sarah we have learned to love,
sweetly lyrical, deeply moralizing. But her touch is unsure.
"A onion, a lettuce" is weak, some of the lines do not quite
scan, and her rhyming of "visible" with "contemplation"
is not in the best traditions of Saskatchewan literature. But
hearken to Sarah six months later:

ODE TO SPRING

'Tis not for long the bird shall creep
Beneath a pile of mouldy straw;
Eftsoons, not long the chill winds sweep,
And powdered snow-bank four feet deep,

Pile up, pile up, in roundish heap:
For spring is coming with its mirth,
And breezy breath of balmy warmth,
And burbank, bobolink, and snearth,[1]
Shall banish winter's chill and dearth,
And luscious joy shall fill the earth.

The poem created a furore when it first appeared. The editor of *The Horsebreeder's Gazette* who finally accepted it for publication gave it the prominence it so richly deserved. Moreover it struck a deeply sympathetic chord in the hearts of the Saskatchewan people. It had been a backward spring. The roads were blocked, and the home-made thermometers were still registering nightly low temperatures of sixty-eight to seventy-five below zero. Suddenly the voice of Sarah, Sarah Binks, the Sweet Songstress, burst upon them with its message of hope and cheer. Spring was coming; the burbank would be back and the return of the snearth was imminent. No wonder Saskatchewan took her to its broad, flat bosom. Two weeks later a delayed chinook melted the Saskatchewan snows and Sarah awoke to find herself, if not exactly famous, at least something of a local celebrity.

It is difficult, if not impossible, to estimate the effect which the success of *Ode to Spring* must have had upon the young poetess. The reception accorded *The Parson's Patch* had been, if not exactly cold, at least disappointing from Sarah's point of view. *The Hitching Post*, where *The Parson's Patch* first appeared, accepted poetical contributions only when accompanied by six fully paid up subscriptions, and the selling of these had tended to lessen Sarah's confidence in herself and in her own poetic ability. Moreover, when finally published it had been wedged in between the obituary notices and the half-page advertisement of a recently discovered cure for harness galls and spavin. But with the appearance of *The Ode* Sarah's confidence returned. Letters of congratulation poured in from Ole and Mathilda, and the editor of *The Fertilizer* personally sent her a form letter calling attention to the fact that his columns were open to all subscribers.

---

[1] It is interesting to note here that this is the first recorded instance of the appearance of the snearth in Saskatchewan. Sarah was always a keen observer of nature.

It has been said that Mathilda served rather as a foil and as an occasion for Sarah's poems than as an actual source of inspiration. This is true in a modified sense. Mathilda herself was not one to inspire a lyrical outburst. It is true that she had that singularly soulful and far-away expression that people who are slightly cross-eyed so often have. She was teeming with health and the pink of the early ripe tomato was in her cheeks. But her features were slightly out of drawing, and she was always, and is still said to be, somewhat large for her age. She tended consequently to be sluggish in her movements, or it may have been that Sarah, always fleet of foot, merely so regarded her, for she herself was less eager to be caught when they played with Ole the simple games of "Auntie, Ante up!" or "Catch-as-catch-can," between the barns and the buggy-shed on Sunday afternoons. However, Mathilda's precocity of size tended towards precocity of mind in some directions, and Sarah found her friend, if not an object of spiritual and sylph-like beauty, at least one of fascinating and absorbing interest. Probably in the end she knew more about Mathilda than Mathilda knew about herself; certainly with Ole's assistance, she knew more about Mathilda than the latter ever suspected. And Mathilda admired Sarah and hung upon her every word, but the somewhat Johnson-Boswellian friendship was in reverse English, and it was Sarah, in this case, who immortalized her admirer in that group or suite of poems which has come to be known as *The Grizzlykick Symphony.*

It is not within the scope of this volume to make a detailed analysis of the Grizzlykick suite of poems. So much has been said and so much has been written about this collection of sweetly tender love lyrics, that anything the Author can add must necessarily be regarded as superfluous. Miss Rosalind Drool in particular has made the greatest contribution to the understanding and appreciation of the *Grizzlykick Symphony.*[1] But no serious study of the life and works of Sarah Binks can ever be complete without some consideration of the throbbing, pulsating, almost nauseating beauty which permeates every line and letter of this famous group, and to the throbbing, pulsating circumstances which brought them about.

---

[1] R. Drool, *The Prairie Crocus and the Passion Flower.* Bunnybooks Ltd. 1933.

4

The Grizzlykick Symphony

AMONG THE SEVERAL admirers of Mathilda Schwantzhacker was Stemka Gryczlkaeiouc (pronounced Grizzlykick), and known in Willows, and more particularly at the Commercial House, as "Stem." Gryczlkaeiouc was a farmer of parts, and owned two quarter sections of land eight miles south of Willows. He lived with his widowed father, Stoompka, or "Stump" Gryczlkaeiouc, who owned the other two quarter sections. Between them, Stump and Stem were thus the owners in fee simple of a complete square mile of Saskatchewan prairie, and could have owned a great deal more if they had thought it worth their while. But having regard for the fact that by all standards of their forefathers they were barons and landowners on a large scale, a fact of which their relatives in the old country were duly apprised from time to time, and having regard also for the cost of barbed wire which had never enclosed their estate, but for fifteen years had merely marked the eastern boundary of it, they were content to rest upon their investment. Although they had never actually succeeded in raising a crop, owing perhaps to the fact that the land south of Willows tended to merge by a series of gentle rises into a low range of sand hills of which their landed property marked the summit, they nevertheless produced some barley and potatoes. These, together with an excellent spring of cold water which the farm miraculously provided, served the elder Gryczlkaeiouc in the production of new beverages in which he was interested, whereas the younger Stemka Gryczlkaeiouc (or Steve Grizzlykick as he came to spell it) gave himself up during the summer months to the joys of the chase. The farm provided excellent hunting, and Stem, always a keen and ardent hunter, albeit a farsighted conservationist in that he seldom actually killed his gophers unless in self-defence, but merely removed the tails, was thus able to count on a steady income from the bounty on gopher tails without impoverishing the land.

It was for Stemka or Steve Grizzlykick and Mathilda Schwantzhacker that the famous *Grizzlykick Symphony* of poems came to be written. Of the meeting of these two souls, of the prairie idyll which led to their marriage and eventually blossomed into love we know all too little. Mathilda herself has aways been reticent about this period, whereas Steve Grizzlykick has not been reticent enough. Marrowfat,[1] it is true, has made an intensive study here and has published his findings without greatly enriching our knowledge of the subject. We are, however, not so much concerned with Steve and Mathilda as we are with Sarah's reactions towards them.

For the poetess, the idyll between Steve and Mathilda was at once an awakening and an opportunity; an awakening in that never before had she attempted to express the tender passion, and an opportunity to express the soul at a new elevation. Her dearest friend was in love and was to be married. It is true, as events showed, that Mathilda at this time was not exactly in love, nor was it for a number of years that she could be called exactly married but all was grist for Sarah's mill. If the path of true love failed to run smoothly all the easier for her metre. She wrote of their meetings, their joys, and their sorrows, their longings and their frustrations. It has even been suggested that she wrote some of the verses for Steve Grizzlykick to hand to Mathilda as his own. This, however, is unlikely. Sarah was too much of the self-conscious artist to trust her genius into strange hands where it might be misinterpreted. She possessed above all the true artist's ability to project herself into another personality and into another situation and make them her own. It is on this basis that the *Grizzlykick Symphony*, as well as all Sarah's poetry, must be understood and appreciated for its true greatness.

The meeting between Steve and Mathilda took place

---

[1] H. Marrowfat, *The Prairie Crocus and the Bologny Flower*, A *Reply to Miss Drool.*—Privately printed and distributed, 1933.

apparently at the schoolhouse dance. There is some evidence to indicate that Steve had seen Mathilda before this occasion and had admired her from afar. The poem *Hi, Sooky, Ho, Sooky*, which was found among Sarah's letters when they were acquired for the Binksian collection, although not in Sarah's handwriting, is obviously in Sarah's inimitable style.

HI, SOOKY, HO, SOOKY

Oh, I heard your voice at daybreak,
Calling loud and sweet and clear;
I was hiding in the turnips
With a cricket in my ear;
A miller-moth in one ear,
And a cricket in the other,
But I heard your dear voice calling
To the piglets and their mother;
Heard your own voice rising, falling,
Loud and long, and sharp and shrill,
Calling, "Sooky, Sooky, Sooky!"
To the piglets on the hill;
   "Hi, Sooky, ho, Sooky,
   Come and get your swill!"

Oh, I've hid among the turnips,
And I've hid between the stooks,
With barley barbs all down my back,
And beetles in my boots;
But I've seen you in the dwindling,
And I've seen you in the rain,
With an armful full of kindling,
When you fell and rose again;
I've seen you plodding through the dust
And plugging through the wet,
And at night against the window-blind,
I've seen your silhouette;
But "Sooky, Sooky, Sooky,"
I never can forget;
   "Hi, Sooky, Ho Sooky,
   Come and get your pep!"

And oh, I think I'll hide again
For just a sight of you,
And hear your own sweet voice again
Call "Sooky, Sooky, Soo,
　　Hi, Sooky, Ho, Sooky,
　　Come and get the stew, Sooky,
　　Come and get your goo, Sooky,
　　Sooky, Sooky, Soo!"

It is a long poem for Sarah. As a rule she expresses herself in a few short verses, leaving the rest to the reader's imagination, and herein, as her commentators are fond of pointing out, lies her greatest charm. Nevertheless, Professor Marrowfat rates it as one of her finest: "Another poem like this and Sarah could give the whole hey-nonny-nonny school of poets Aces and Jacks."

Concerning the dance where Steve is supposed to have met Mathilda, we have two poems. In *Invitation to the Dance* Sarah has captured the lilt and rhythm of the dance itself:

INVITATION TO THE DANCE

Come tread me the measure,
I give you the pleasure,
The one-step, the two-step, or three,
The polka so tender,
You'll always remember,
With joy if you tread it with me.

You'll be glad that we met—
To the clarionette
We will swing and we'll twist on the floor,
With a bound we will mount,
To the middle and count—
One-two-three, one-two-three, four.

In *The Meeting* Sarah expresses the ecstatic joy of a young man on meeting his beloved for the first time:

THE MEETING

Dearest, can I forget that day of meeting,
'Twas at a dance—I diffidently threw
A conversation lozenge for a greeting—
It hit you in the eye, my aim was true;
You dropped your cup of coffee, I remember,
You blushed and rose and gave me playful shove,
And oh, that look, beyond description tender,
With one eye closed and one eye full of love;
I offered you my armband as a token,
Complete with photograph—you took it slow,
Reluctantly—you said it might get broken,
But thought you'd wear it where it wouldn't show;
And I, who drank of life's abounding measure,
Shall hold your token as a thing apart—
The sandwich that you gave me I shall treasure,
And wear it always closest to my heart.

Love ripens quickly in the dry air of Saskatchewan. Two days after *The Meeting* Sarah reached a new high in *The Plight*, a poem in which the shy flutterings of Mathilda's heart for Steve Grizzlykick are expressed in the symbolism of the tree. Trees were always scarce around Willows and tended to be small; the oldest, and in fact, the only tree [1] between Willows and South Vigil, and undoubtedly the one mentioned in *The Plight* is still of such a size that to enjoy its shade is a matter attended by difficulty. *The Plight* is therefore doubly interesting in that it represents a botanical as well as lyrical achievement.

THE PLIGHT

Is this the tree that saw our first love's plighting,
And those the leaves that heard our first love's vow,
And yonder limb that saw love's first delighting,
Is that the very limb, the self-same bough?

---

[1] This tree finally died during the drought of 1937. The bronze plate mounted thereon by the Ladies' Literary League of Quagmire in commemoration of Rover has since been removed and is preserved in their collection of Binksiana.

Is this its scanty shade where love first hit me,
And caterpillars tumbled from on high;
Is yonder ant the very ant that bit me,
And them the same mosquitoes in the sky?

Can this then be the tree that seemed so leaden,
And grey and dull a scant few hours ago?
Now all is changed; its branches reach to heaven,
And up and down the angel antlets go;
Time cannot change, though leaf and twig may wither,
And caterpillar struggle into moth.
This is the tree that heard love's first sweet blither,
This is the spot we loudly plighted troth.

Sarah has written many charming poems in her time, but
for airy lightness none perhaps touches in charm that uni-
versal favourite *The Wedding Dress*. It would appear that
Mathilda was already considering her trousseau and in defiance of the Schwantzhacker tradition, is about to order
one from the mail order catalogue. Her even greater defiance
of the tradition that a dress must not shrink, and must "wear,
wash, and be warm," may be due to Sarah's influence. Dr
Mahal also points out, with his usual mathematical accuracy,
that dresses at that time were four inches shorter than the
present mean length.

THE WEDDING DRESS

On page two hundred and sixty three,
Oh, there's the very dress for me,
    The price is right,
    The size is tight,
The colour red, and green, and white,
And I'll be chick, I'll be petite,
    Oh, that's the dress for me!

They say that man wants little here,
Nor wants that little long—nor dear,
    And so I say,
    On wedding day,
A dress that's short, and cute, and gay,
And light enough for the breeze to play,
    And a special price "To clear."

Though after wedding day we find
It's short in front and long behind,
      And winds on heath
      Get underneath,
And rattle bones, and ribs. and teeth.
For wedding day with wedding wreath
      I want to look refined.

It may have been that Sarah, carried away by her poetical imagination, anticipated somewhat when she wrote *Proposal* and *Christmas Eve*, two songs which glorify the wedding day. The computations of Dr Taj Mahal would indicate that these two poems, together with *Lullaby*, were written at a later date, although Marrowfat, whose contempt for the mathematical interpretation of literature is equalled only by that which he entertains for the Literary Editor of the *Farm and Fair*, points to the internal evidence of *Proposal* in refutation. Steve apparently, during the closed season for gophers, was in the habit of hiring himself out for a week or so at a time, and consequently appears in the *Proposal* as a hired man.

PROPOSAL

The hired man to the maiden spoke;
"Oh, marry me tomorrow,
We'll fill the heater up with coke,
Kettle, beans, and bacon borrow,
Make a table, build a bed—
Who so happy when we're wed?
      Happy, happy, while we can,"
      To the maid the hired man.

"Oh, not so fast," the maid replied,
"In this I am immutable,
I fear your love would weaken,
Though your ardour's indisputable;
Love may wane and love may wax,
Mine can only thrive on facts.
      Work a year and we shall see,"
      Cried the maiden modestly.

Apparently the path of true love was already beginning to deviate from a straight line. There is, however, little to indicate this in *Lullaby*, one of Sarah's finest. This lullaby has been included in the recently published *Anthology of British Lullabies Since 1900*. Lord Inchworm, in his preface to this anthology, comments as follows: "The British Empire has produced some very sweet lullabies in its day, but for sheer opiate and saccharine quality few have excelled that of the Canadian poetess Sarah Binks. I have never yet succeeded in reading it through; the last time I started it I fell asleep and slept like a child for hours afterwards."

LULLABY

Sleep, my darling, sleep away,
Daddy's gone to town with hay,
And at four o'clock will come
The man who sells aluminum;
Mother's sold on kitchen ware,
Sleep, she wants to do her hair.
Though you're far too young for telling,
Mother doesn't want you yelling
When the salesman comes—so you,
Sleep 'till five or a quarter to.

Sleep, my precious, close your eyes,
Mother's sold on plates for pies,
And tomorrow—go to sleep—
Daddy goes to town with sheep,
Better count them while you're able,
When they're gone they'll lock the stable,
So we'll count them, you and me,
Four o'clock comes after three.
Count the hours, count the sheep.
Sleep, you little nuisance, sleep.

In *Christmas Eve* we find Sarah singing the joys of the wedding day with a full throat:

CHRISTMAS EVE

When birthday comes on Christmas Eve,
And Christmas Eve is bridal night,
The maiden's heart is filled with joy,
She bounces with delight;
    For wedding day at last is here,
    And Christmas comes but once a year.

And at her hand the bashful groom
Is happy in her pledge,
He plucks the fairest flowers that bloom,
From off the window ledge;
    With joy he lays them at her feet,
    And gazes loving, long, and sweet.

Oh, may that day be bright and gay,
With laughter loud, and chuckle,
No evil unkind fate hold sway
To rend the veil and buckle;
    Each wedding and each birthday leave
    A kindly thought for Christmas Eve!

In this poem Sarah undoubtedly anticipates events. Several Christmas Eves and more than one birthday were to pass for Mathilda before the "wedding day at last is here." The short poem beginning

> Soon old Steve will have to build a
> Two-room shanty for Mathilda . . .

is not indicative of the actual events, and, moreover, has never been admitted as one of Sarah's works, but has been variously ascribed to Ole, or to any one of the thirteen Schwantzhacker sisters. It was found written on one of the buildings of the Binks's farm. The original manuscript was carefully sawn off and through the kindness of the Rack Loan and Holding Company, owners of the original mortgage on N. E. ¼ Sec. 37, T.21, R.9 W., in charging only for the actual material and labour and cartage, found its way into the collection of Binksiana, but it was inadvertently removed from its glass case and used for kindling by the curator, when he was making the morning fire in the adjoining rest room.

The cause of the break between Steve and Mathilda which delayed their union by so many years is not definitely known. Various hypotheses have been advanced, one of the most ingenious of which [1] is that Steve in his new found happiness took to drinking heavily. But this hypothesis is not in keeping with the character of Mathilda, nor of the countryside. One need only read Sarah's The Pledge to realize that Steve's well-known fondness for the wines native to Willows enhanced him in Mathilda's eyes. Professor Marrowfat, in laborious preparation for a brochure on the native wines and cheeses of Saskatchewan, has made a very exhaustive study of the particular wine mentioned as "applejack" in The Pledge and gives several recipes for its preparation. He points out, however, that the name "applejack" is really a misnomer, in that the wine is not made from apples but from potatoes, and derives its flavour from the addition of a pound of evaporated apples to each ten gallons of mash. Sometimes a few sprigs of dill and a very small quantity of rough-on-rats was added when a liqueur and tonic for the aged was required. The poet, however, speaks always in the language of the people, and although The Pledge is written in the heroic manner, Sarah is too much the voice of Saskatchewan not to call it applejack.

The Pledge tells in language ever new the age-long story of a young man (Steve) taking leave of his beloved on the eve of battle.

THE PLEDGE

Mathilda, fair, to Thee I pledge
    This cup of applejack;
I drink—and should I fall tonight,
    Weep not, nor hold me back.

Weep not, my own, though mine own eyes
    May fail, my footsteps falter,
Weep not, I rise again and sing
    To tambour sound and psalter;

---

[1] Marrowfat, Native Wines and Cheeses of the American North-West. Bull. Ed. Sask. No. 1.

Like others sang, and others tried,
    With flowing bowl to grapple,
Theirs was the song of purple grape,
    Mine the song of apple.

Mathilda, mine, to thee this cup,
    And once again I pledge,
And still again; this night may see
    Me lie beneath the hedge;

Beneath the hedge and open sky,
    And oh, the dawn's bright breaking
May find me in stentorious sleep
    Until that long sleep's waking.

A. S. Toreador, writing in a recent issue of *The Book-worm*, says of this poem: "The soil of Saskatchewan has been enriched and fertilized by this song. It is the very breath of the people...."

5

William Greenglow

To WILLIAM GREENGLOW, geologist and educationist, goes the honour and credit of introducing Sarah Binks to the great science of geology. No less person than the Honourable A. E. Windheaver, Minister of Foreign Affairs and Grasshopper Control, speaking before an audience of almost three hundred people, pays him tribute. The closing lines of his peroration, as reported by the special correspondent of the Pelvis, Sask., *Banner*, run as follows:

> Literary movements grow, fashions change, and people leave the country. But geology is founded upon a rock. The great Liberal party, which I have the honour to represent and which is not responsible for these roads, may some day pass away. But when that day comes, and I say it advisedly, when that day comes, the price of wheat will be down to twenty cents, f.o.b. Fort William, the fodder crops will rot in the fields, and these here roads will be the home of the rearing cactus and the gopher. The Liberal party has always fought against that type of thing. But when that day comes, I want to say that geology will still be geology. The big interests of Ontario and Quebec that are trying to run this great country of yours and are keeping down the price of steers, will bump against the rock of geology. We've got the whole north country unexplored and undeveloped. Think of it! Over four million square miles of solid rock. And we are going to use that money to put the agriculture of Saskatchewan on a solid footing. We, who have gathered here today to honour the memory of Sarah Binks, your local girl,

the light of whose gem shines brightest in the diadem of this City of Willows, and of whom the Government is so justly proud, we must never forget that geology played a part in her life also, and that William Greenglow, who first taught her the rudiments of this science, was at the same time the first practical geologist of this great Province.

This tribute to Greenglow, coming as it does from so eminent a statesman as the Hon. A. E. Windheaver, himself no mean geologist, as his armorial bearings of pick, shovel and salt shaker upon the engraved stock certificates show, and uttered upon the occasion of the Sarah Festival and Basket Picnic at Willow View Park, shows how profoundly Greenglow's influence extends, and how deeply Sarah penetrates into the soil of Saskatchewan. "She expresses," according to the Literary Editor of *The Horsebreeder's Gazette*, "not only the soul of Saskatchewan, but its very bones; the Jurassic, Triassic, or the plain Assic, are all there. She puts the Carboniferous up to us."

It is not the intention of the Author of this study to go into the geology of Saskatchewan. But no one can understand Sarah's poems in their deeper meaning, and in particular her later poems, without some knowledge of that oil boom and geological wave of activity which swept the Willows district during the summer in which William Greenglow taught at the Willows School.

Of William Greenglow's antecedents we know surprisingly little. Manitoba has claimed him as a native son but has also disclaimed him. It is difficult to decide. That he was a student at St Midget's College is known, but owing to the fact that his fees at that institution have not been completely paid, his academic record is not available. According to his own records, in which he tended to become confused and which tend accordingly to be unreliable, he had obtained a total of ten and a half units, fourteen credits, eleven and five-sixteenth pundits during the first term of the second half of the first division, and by transferring three digits from the diploma course to the degree course of the second division, he would have a total of twenty three half-credits, which would entitle him to the degree of Jack of Arts, leaving six marklets, or one semi-microbe, which could later be counted towards the degree of Bachelor of Arts. There is, however, no record of his having obtained either of these degrees although on the prospectuses of various companies with which he has been associated, he appears with the letters J.A. after is name. Perhaps if he had not been conditioned in elementary geology and had paid his fees he would have received his degree at least extramurally. "What a pity," writes Dean Pindle, "that a man like him has to go through life without an education. The Senate would finally have passed him in geology if he had only paid his fees."

But St Midget's loss was Sarah's gain. It was this very condition in geology which brought Greenglow to Saskatchewan. Having written it twice and been thrown for a greater loss of half-credits on each occasion, not to mention the greater loss of complete credit with his landlady, he had obtained, through the medium of his uncle and an application of the Minister of Education, a temporary permit to teach school in either the "unorganized" or "disorganized" schools of Saskatchewan. And being resolved to repair his mental as well as his financial standing, he had brought with him only his textbook in geology, putting, as he himself admitted, "all other books out of temptation."

The result of this singular concentration of effort was to shed a greater flood of geological light into the community of Willows than into the community of William Greenglow's mind. In this respect he must be regarded as a true educator if not a great one, for he had the educator's peculiar genius for imparting knowledge without himself assimilating it. Few teachers in the history of education in Saskatchewan have excelled him in this respect. Information flowed from him, to use the apt phrasing of Jacob Binks, "like beer from a spigot", and like a spigot he could turn it off at four o'clock without permitting any inertial flow to carry him beyond his duties. It is true that he frequently kept Mathilda after school, but this, as he explained to the school board, was because he was "not satisfied with her progress," and could hardly be regarded as violating the wishes of the school board against the too zealous enthusiasm for mere book learning.

William Greenglow's educational policy was to teach his class geology and at the same time have them teach it to him. That he failed in the latter respect was due not so much to his pedagogical method, attended with so much success elsewhere, as to the fact that only one copy of the text was available for the use of the school. If two copies of Warden and Rockbuster's *First Steps in Geology* had been available, one for the teacher and one for the class, Greenglow would have been able to follow the recitations and the lessons in reading with greater accuracy. Always an educator, he felt that his first duty was towards his class and consequently he had little time during school hours to peruse the volume himself. But in spite of the handicap of the teacher it was a golden age for the pupils. Greenglow himself characterizes the happy combination of geological and pedagogical methods as one of outstanding success: "They are drilled but never bored," he writes in one of his letters, "and a good time is had by all." He continues:

They take to geology like the Board of Trade. I have divided the school into a Junior Division and a Senior Division. At present the Junior Division is out on practical work, classifying the field boulders into big ones, little ones and in between ones, thereby earning units and credits. Only half of the Senior Division is present this afternoon and there wouldn't even be that if I hadn't promoted her from Junior to Senior Division last week. That's Mathilda. And boy, oh boy, does that baby know her geology!

The other half of the Senior Division is the Binks girl. She is probably helping her old man with the haying these days, or off writing another poem. I lent her my copy of Warden and Rockbuster the other day to take home. Never again. She lent it to Ole, who took it into the field, and two of the pages are missing, fortunately not the ones containing my last year's notes. She offered to pay for them on a *pro rata* basis, but there are two hundred pages in the book, so I said I would let her have the whole thing for fifty cents if she would let us use it in the school until the fall. Old Sage, her grandfather, came round last night and closed the deal.

It is apparent that the personal influence of William Greenglow upon Sarah, the poetess, was by no means as great as upon Mathilda. But his literary influence through the medium of his teaching can hardly be overestimated. She strikes at once the new note. One moment she is lyrical, gay, as in her *Song to the Four Seasons*, the next moment she is deep in the fossil beds of the Ordovician or the Preluvian. One moment she sings the joy of the farmer's life, catches in her web of poesy the ephemeral dust storm and imprints it indelibly upon the hearts of men, the next moment she is down to hard-pan, struggling with new forms, mastering new material. Early in June she wrote those two flawless gems *Song to the Four Seasons* and *The Farmer and the Farmer's Wife*. Two weeks later she began that great Epic, or "Super Poem", which she later revised and enlarged and finally completed under the title, *Up from the Magma and Back Again*. Strictly speaking this great opus belongs to a later period of her life. It is not suggested that the thirteen cantos or even the Prologue were completed at this period. But they were conceived and began to take form. We know for certain that the lines—

> Should maddened pterodactyl chance to meet
> With raging crocodile,
> Then crocodile the pterodactyl eat,
> Or pterodactyl eat the crocodile,

—lines which occur again and again throughout the epic as well as in the Epilogue, were written around this time. Moreover the quatrain

> Man, who is creature of the moment jist,
> Is yet a fossil in micaceous schist,
> Tomorrow's day, his bones are bleached and bent,
> A something for the archaeologist,

was written the same summer, although it was not until some years later, in fact after she had been to Regina, that she was to add those famous lines which gave the verse its completeness;

> Man who has spurned and made my heart to hurt,
> Is but a creature and a thing of dirt,
> A thing of mud, of clay, volcanic ash,
> Old brick, cinders, broken cement, chert.

The geological motive is very strong here. It was to follow her all her life. Not only her poems, but her very conversation takes on the geological flavour. She refers to her grandfather as "sedimentary" in his habits; Ole's expression is affectionately described on one occasion as being somewhat "palaeozoic" in character, and she refers to the first glacial period as if it were the winter before last. She sends a message to the Schwantzhacker sisters in which they are aptly and picturesquely addressed as "trilobites." Sarah was never at a loss for the correct word.

But in spite of this strong geological influence which had entered her life and through her the literature of Saskatchewan, she never loses her joy in the sweet simplicity of the Saskatchewan scene. The pastoral influence was too strong. Heaken to Sarah as she sings her *Song to the Four Seasons* :

Spring is here, the breezes blowing,
Four inches of top-soil going, going;
Farm ducks rolling across the prairie;
Spring is here—how nice and airy!

Summer has come, the hoppers are back,
The sun shines bright, the fields shine black,
Cloudlets gather, it looks like rain—
Ah, the patter of hail on the window pane!

Bounteous harvest, we'll sell at cost—
Tomorrow we'll have an early frost;
Glorious autumn, red with rust;
We'll live on the general store on trust.

A long, quiet winter with plenty of snow,
And plenty of barley; it's eighty below,
Barley in the heater, salt pork in the pantry—
How nice that you never feel cold in this country.[1]

Greenglow mentions in his letter that Sarah was probably helping her father with the haying or "off writing another

---

[1] It is in rhymes such as these, "country" made to rhyme with "pantry" that Sarah reveals herself as a daughter of the Old South.

poem". Probably she was doing both with her chief attention on the poem. We know from Ole's account of an incident that one day she buried Grandfather Thurnow so deeply in the hay that he might conceivably be there yet had she not been fortunate enough to discover him while pressing down the hay with the pitchfork. The incident may have wearied her of haying. Certainly it is with relief that she lays down the tool on Saturday night and expresses the joy of girlhood set free in those lines *Tomorrow Is Sunday*.

Hang up the pitchfork, another week over!
The weeks all end, and they all begin;
But tomorrow for me, and for Ole and Rover,
It's Sunday—and Sunday we all sleep in.

Tonight we go shopping, we'll bring home some butter,
Canned milk and eggs from the general store,
Visitors coming tomorrow—it's Sunday,
And Sunday an extra hour to snore.

Tomorrow is Sunday, bright and breezy,
We'll cook four meals to keep alive,
And do the chores, but we'll take it easy,
For tomorrow is Sunday—we'll sleep 'til five.

Another week's ploughing and haying and seeding,
Another wash-day has come and gone,
Another day's sewing and baking and weeding,
But tomorrow is Sunday, we'll sleep 'til dawn.[1]

By Monday she is hard at it again; it may have been that the Sunday visitors intruding into her dreams and her solitude wearied her more than the haying, at least we find her once more hymning the praises of the pastoral life. Before midsummer she had completed *The Farmer and the Farmer's Wife*. It is one of the greatest of her short poems. It was first published in the Piecemeal *Excelsior*, but was immediately

---

[1] These lines were recently quoted with telling effect by Augustus Windheaver Jr., heading the annual delegation to the Dominion Government with the petition to have the Willows-Quagmire district formed into a separate province. He declared, 'Daylight saving means secession."

copied by *The Times* of Protuberance, Sask., and *The Beam*, of Vigil, N. W. T. She received no royalties from this piracy of an author's rights, but she expected none at this stage of her career. Hers were still the pleasures of giving. She did, however, write to the manager of the Lax Cosmetics Company at Saskatoon, who had used some of her lines in one of their advertisements, calling attention to the fact that her name was spelled with an I instead of a U, but received no reply.

THE FARMER AND THE FARMER'S WIFE

The farmer and the farmer's wife
Lead frolicsome and carefree lives,
And all their work is but in play,
Their labours only exercise.

The farmer leaps from bed to board,
And board to binder on the land;
His wife awakes with shouts of joy,
And milks a cow with either hand.

Then all in fun they feed the pigs,
And plough the soil in reckless glee,
And play the quaint old-fashioned game
Of mortgagor and mortgagee.

And all day long they dash about,
In barn and pasture, field and heath;
He sings a merry roundelay,
She whistles gaily through her teeth.

And when at night the chores are done,
And hand in hand they sit and beam,
He helps himself to applejack,
And she to Paris Green.

The Farmer and the Farmer's Wife stands pre-eminent in the annals of Saskatchewan lyricism. Marrowfat gives it his unstinted praise. He says in part: "I like The Farmer's Wife. She starts out well and ends on a high note." Inspector Peeker, probably the most outstanding critic in several school districts, says of this poem : "The teachers of Baal and Cactus Lake have asked that this poem be put on the list of supplementary reading."

The fact that Sarah, through the good influences and financial assistance of Grandfather Thurnow, now had an option on the single textbook in Geology, entitled her to its exclusive use on those days when she attended school. William Greenglow, more concerned with Mathilda's education than with Sarah's, found this arrangement an admirable one. Mathilda had been finding difficulty in understanding the theory of crustal movements, and the teacher was now able to give more time to this fascinating subject, while Sarah devoted herself to the larger outlook. It was a formative period in her education; scholars aptly refer to it as the Neo-Plasticine.

Sarah was undoubtedly the founder of the geo-literary school of poetry. Her position in that respect has never been questioned.[1] But the Author of this great work goes even further, in venturing the suggestion that if geology influenced Sarah, then Sarah in turn influenced geology, at least the geology of Saskatchewan. One need only read *Up from the Magma and Back Again*, and compare its swift cavalcade of events in the thirteenth Canto with those that actually occurred around Willows, to appreciate the truth on which this hypothesis rests. Actually few critics who profess to be familiar with Sarah Binks's works have read *Up from the Magma* from end to end. Marrowfat never gets beyond the chorus of the trilobites, and the always mathematical Doctor Taj Mahal admits that so far he has merely counted the number of lines, and is working on the number of letters. But if the *Magma* is ever completely read, the truth will become at once apparent. The whole Heavenly scene of the thirteenth Canto even to the four elevators, is strangely reminiscent of Willows. Moreover some of the names and characters are but thinly disguised; Rover has his counterpart in that mysterious

---

[1] Mr Ram Spud, (apologies to Leacock) later Sir Ramshorn Spud, one of the great Untouchables of India, in comparing Sarah's *Up from the Magma*, with his own *Parabolas in Sanscrit* claims this honour, and more, for himself. He states, "I alone am the father of the Neo-Geo-literary school." Dr Taj Mahal supports his countryman in this, but both make the same mistake in confusing geology with astrology.

animal, Strover, Ole becomes Sir Pontifex Lowly, the thirteen Schwantzhacker sisters reappear as the thirteen trilobites, and the connection between Henry Beltpin and Henry Welkin is almost too obvious to be missed. Throughout this celestial scene stalks the Muse, Salacia, making notes, referring to the book which she carries under her arm, putting the trilobites in their places, and telling the angels where to dig. So also when the great oil boom drifted eastward from Alberta and finally reached Willows, Sarah, almost as much as William Greenglow, took charge.

The discovery of indications of oil near Willows has already been recorded in *The Claim Jumper*, the official organ of the Quagmire Bureau of Mines. The actual discovery, although officially in William Greenglow's name, must also be credited to Mathilda. Like so many discoveries of this nature it was entirely accidental. Greenglow himself had been searching for indications of oil for some time, having been commissioned to do so by the management of the Millenium Development and Exploration Company, who spurred him on to even greater effort by the inducement that he would be made their field geologist for that district as soon as the indications of oil had been discovered. His first day's effort had proven entirely fruitless; it was not until the evening that he recalled a spot a rod or two to the rear of the Binks' barn where he remembered having once detected signs of seepage. Fate, however, seems to have played strange tricks. Had he followed his original intention he might have discovered seepage, but he would certainly not have discovered oil. He hesitated, and prompted by some obscure voice, or his own unfailing instinct, he turned in the opposite direction. Precisely at the spot where for several years the separator had been standing, and where Mathilda had more than once suggested that it might be worth his while to look, he discovered the first indications of oil.

The location of the discovery claim as shown in the sketch map of William Greenglow's field notes, does not coincide with the spot where the first shaft was sunk. Ole obligingly enough, pulled the separator out of the way, but Jacob Binks' peremptory, "Take that dam' separator back where you found it" restored it to its original site. Jacob Binks, first and always the dirt farmer, was not the kind to have his landscape changed and his scenes shifted without protest. He gave his consent to drilling operations when the possibility of a water supply for the stock was pointed out to him, but otherwise he intended to remain, as Sarah puts it, "crustaceous". The location of the well was therefore shifted under Sarah's direction several times until a suitable spot was found safe from the meanderings of the perennial calf and, if possible, out of the line of Ole's route from town on Saturday nights.

Oil in paying quantities was never obtained from the well which was finally sunk. The citizens of Willows, who had subscribed to the shares of the subsidiary company formed for the purpose of this development, were no more disappointed than the Millenium Company itself. This Company pointed out later that if Ole had been permitted to move the separator from the original claim, the oil beds might have been reached from that point. As it was, three separate shafts were begun with Ole's post-hole auger before the final or main shaft was developed. The first shaft struck a placer deposit of harrow teeth at the three foot level, but was not rich enough to warrant further development at the time and was abandoned. In the second shaft the Pre-Cambrian Shield, or what Greenglow took to be the Pre-Cambrian Shield, was reached at a depth of fifteen feet. Hopes ran high. In the Pre-Cambrian Shield oil might reasonably be expected at any moment. Anything can happen in the Pre-Cambrian Shield. If not oil then beryllium, and if not beryllium then bolognium. It was Sarah, poking down the shaft with a long stick, who made the important discovery that what Greenglow took to be the Pre-Cambrian Shield was an unusually large field boulder and that although Ole could be sent down to hand it up, others might be encountered at a lower level and that the shaft had better be abandoned in favour of another site visible from the kitchen window.

The third well, and the most successful one, was the one which finally yielded the gusher. Sarah was by this time practically in charge of the operations, although William Greenglow was officially the field geologist. An argument amounting almost to a dispute arose between the two as to the location of the third borings. Greenglow's intention was to go almost straight down until the Upper Silurian was reached and then either to penetrate this formation or go around it. Sarah, however, pointed out to him that what he took to be a syncline in the Upper Silurian was in fact the back side of the anticline between the Preluvian and the Lower Galician and that the well should be moved at least forty rods due west. Greenglow, who was now determined to leave no stone unturned in his search for oil, agreed to give it a trial, but conceded the point so reluctantly that had it not been for Jacob Binks' objection that these continual borings were hard on the land, it is possible that a fourth well might have been attempted.

The gusher was struck towards morning on the third day at the forty-five foot level. It lay, as Sarah had predicted, in the intermediate horizon between the Preluvian and the Lower Galician. The dramatic episode is faithfully described in *Up from the Magma and Back Again*. In the *Magma* the thirteen trilobites are pictured as gathered around when the gusher is struck and are drenched to the skin, subsequently catching cold from exposure. In actual fact none of the thirteen Schwantzhacker sisters, with the possible exception of Mathilda, was present at the time, having left for home an hour earlier on learning from the crew of the night shift that no further developments were to be expected. Moreover, as Marrowfat for once correctly contends, it is unlikely that Mathilda would ever suffer any ill effects from exposure. Sarah takes full advantage of her poetic licence here.

It is poetic licence also which enables Sarah to describe the well as a "gusher". The actual gush, always excepting that of the Millenium Development and Exploration Company, subsided after twenty-five minutes to a mere trickle. The oil content, which William Greenglow's field notes classify as a "smear" were later corrected by more exact chemical analysis to "trace". But if the oil content was disappointingly low, the alkaline content was correspondingly high, and Grandfather Thurnow, quick to appreciate the medicinal value of such a spring, incorporated its waters in his famed formula for wild sage bitters, even going to the trouble and expense of putting down a cistern pump. The curative value of these waters has been described as radioactive, or sometimes retroactive, but always active. It is conceivable that the well might have developed into a spa of international reputation had it not been for the drought. As an oil well it can never rank with those of Turner Valley and Texas; as a well of almost any kind it must be classed with those that were great only in their failure. Jacob Binks may well say as he so often said, ". . . even the dam' steers won't drink it", but we must never forget that from its waters Sarah, poetically and figuratively, and Grandfather Thurnow literally, have "drunk deep". We must never forget that Sarah has done more than plumb its forty-five foot depths. *Up from the Magma and Back Again,* that super epic in thirteen cantos with its prologue and epilogue, could never arise alone from a forty-five foot well, and especially one which, as Taj Mahal points out, is considerably off the perpendicular. Those haunting lines

> Should maddened pterodactyl chance to meet
> With raging crocodile,
> Then crocodile the pterodactyl eat, *etc, etc.*

express more than an oil well. They speak to us of the Upper Silurian. They speak to us of the Lower Galician. They speak to us of the Plasticine, the Preluvian, the overburden, the underburden, the chert concretion, the Great Ice age. Nay, the whole super epic breathes in and breathes out the geological soul of Saskatchewan.

6

The Binks-Thurnow
Controversy

OLE, ROVER, WM. GREENGLOW, Henry Welkin, Thadeus T. Thurnow, what a splendid cavalcade, and all male! It is the very masculinity of their influence which makes Sarah's work so Saskatchewanesque, and where they influenced her life they influenced her work. With the exception of Grandfather Thurnow, who will always be unique, they fall singularly into pairs. Where she took from Ole her sweet simplicity, her love of the pastoral scene, and her oneship with nature, from Greenglow she acquired its tremendous geological sweep. Where from Rover she acquired the mystical note and haunting cadence and mastery of new metrical forms, from Henry Welkin she received those deep shadows, and dark browns with which much of her work is coloured during the Post Regina period. But Thadeus T. (Grandfather) Thurnow stands alone. By all the ties of blood and home and affection his is the greatest influence in that from him Sarah received, if not her genius, at least many of his philosophical genes.

Thadeus T. Thurnow, last of the long line of Thurnows (originally Thurnips) was a figure in the community of Willows. He was noted for his breadth of mind and body, and the fact that he was called "Old Sage" is a tribute as much to the profundity of his wisdom as to his herbal remedies. His beard was long and full, and possessed that property, already becoming so rare, of being what the botanists describe as *branchiate*, in which each hair tends to branch into a series of secondary or even tertiary hairs, much like the root system of the common bunch grass. The result was a beard which resembled the creeping juniper after a heavy frost, except that during the height of its season it tended to resume its original rich loamy colour, and was at all times faintly phosphorescent. This phosphorescence may have been due to his atavistic passion for the juice of turnips, for it has long been known that the soil of Saskatchewan produces a turnip which is particularly rich in turnipin and the turnipinoids, compounds closely related to carotin and the carotinoids which when properly extracted and matured are said to be phosphorescent when mixed with phosphorus. In any case it is known that by its glow Old Sage could find his way home on the darkest night.

He was not a tall man, certainly not compared with Ole, but he was larger than Ole, stone for stone. He had great breadth of shoulder, and the line from the chest down was drawn in a confident arc. In the beam too, his great breadth was indicative of his independence of mind and his tendency towards philosophical contemplation. Figures, of course, are available. They have been discussed at considerable length and some depth under the title, *T. T. Thurnow, A Three Dimensional Study*, by Dr Taj Mahal.

His great wisdom was a legend in the community. Regardless of the subject under discussion he was able to contribute from the wealth of his experiences, or, if these were lacking, parables which bore all the semblance of experiences. In his early days he could speak the language of the Ojibways and of the Mound Builders—in fact he had assimilated much of the red man's obscure philosophy and his knowledge of herbal remedies—and he is known on election day to have given a demonstration of an Indian tribal dance in the Clarendon Hotel at Willows, in which he successively and then simultaneously took the part of every member of the tribe.

In his political opinions he differed little from Jacob Binks. Jacob Binks was a Liberal and patronized the Commercial House, whereas Thadeus T. Thurnow's choice, when it was offered, invariably fell to the Clarendon Hotel. But he was not bigoted and these differences of opinion may have been due not so much to politics as to the fact that the title of the North East Quarter of Section 37, Township 21, Range 9, West, was by this time vested in the name of Thadeus T. Thurnow, which would tend to make the latter, as a landed proprietor, more Conservative in his outlook. Certainly Jacob Binks' characterization of him as "the biggest dam' liar west of the Principal Meridian" was expressed as often in pride as in the heat of political argument, and concerning the farm he was wont to quote Grandfather Thurnow's homely epigram of which the latter had been delivered one day after an hour's argument, *viz.*, "It's the last sardine in the tin gets the olive oil." Undoubtedly Old Sage was too great a man to wear for long any political label, and it is characteristic of the man that after his demise when he was stuffed and mounted and presented to the Nation for the Binksian Collection, and later offered as a candidate to the electors of Quagmire-Willows Constituency by the Liberal Party, he should have failed of election only by being disqualified by the Conservatives who claimed him as a candidate of their own.

Between Sarah and her Grandfather there was a bond of sympathy and understanding and mutual admiration. From her earliest childhood she had sat at his knee and drunk in his wisdom and his philosophy. From him she received her understanding of the cosmos, of time, and of space, but especially of time. To Grandfather Thurnow the three dimensions of space were more than abstractions; they were something to be lived, something to be realized in one's everyday life, and he never departed from this conviction. But in the matter of time he was the complete philosopher. Past, present, and future were inextricably blended, and his mastery of them was such that he was able to use all three interchangeably. When he addresses Sarah as "My son", or refers to Jacob Binks as an "old woman", he is bringing his greatest powers into play. His knowledge of psychology, especially animal psychology, was profound, and undoubtedly Sarah took much of the inspiration of *Horse* from his meditations. Certainly, in the case of Rover, he could, as he admitted, "read him like a book," and in his delineation of the latter's psychology he was sometimes wont to include Mathilda.

In a sense it is almost unfortunate that the bond between Sarah and her Grandfather should have been so firm. That storm, the Binks-Thurnow controversy which has swept the literary circles of Saskatchewan might then never have arisen. But then *Time*, and *Space*, and *Horse*, and *Crisscrossers* might never have been written and Saskatchewan would be the poorer by just that much. It is unfortunate that Professor Marrowfat, in his so-called *Critical Analysis* has raised the question of the authenticity of some of Sarah Binks' poems, and it is even more regrettable that the discussions which followed should have taken on what appears to be a personal note. Certainly the incident between Professor Marrowfat and the literary editor of the *Farm and Fair*, in which the latter is said to have kicked the Professor below the belt and from behind, exceeds the bounds of literary criticism. Nor can Professor Marrowfat's attempt to gouge the literary editor's eye be regarded as a contribution to scholarly research. Nor is it the aim of the Author to decide between the respective merits of the two gentlemen. But Professor Marrowfat's contention as to the authenticity of some of the poems has been a challenge which the Author has finally decided to face squarely.

Professor Marrowfat's contention is based on the internal evidence of the four poems, *Time*, *Space*, *Horse*, and *Criss-crossers*. His argument, in brief, when sifted from the mass of verbiage, bad spelling, and split infinitives, which character-ize all his papers, is that Sarah could not have written these poems, especially *Time* because she lacked the profound philosophical background which characterizes the poems. She was young, she was immature, and she certainly could not have reached that mellow, that ripe, that almost over-ripe wisdom which is the breath and soul of *Time* and *Criss-crossers*. "I don't allow," says Marrowfat,[1] "that Sarah done it. I have had a lot of experience with women, and I have never met one yet who had any idea of time and space except as their personal enemies. They are preoccupied with time and space only insofar as they tend to show, and in-creasingly occupy, these entities, but philosophically—nix!"

On the other hand, there was Thadeus T. Thurnow, pas-sive, meditative, hirsute, full of turnipin, and, as Jacob Binks describes him, "given to setting around". He at least, "had reached the age of ninety-six and with it that Kantian-Ojib-wayan conception of time which is the breath and soul of the poem. It is from his pen, and from his matured brain that

---

[1] Marrowfat, H., *Cosmology and Cosmetics*—Bull. Ed. Sask. No. 2.

the sonorous lines and deep truths must have rolled."
Thadeus T. Thurnow, and not Sarah Binks, Marrowfat maintains,[1] is therefore, the author of *Time*, and *Horse* and *Crisscrossers*, and a number of other poems. In fact, the whole
question of authorship is thrown open to dispute.

It would be easy enough to throw some doubt on the
authority with which Professor Marrowfat speaks by reference to incidents in his private life. But as these, together
with his literary and physical antecedents, have already been
carefully enumerated by the Editor of *Farm and Fair*, let us
examine the internal evidence of *Time* and compare it with
the internal evidence of *Horse*.

TIME

My Son, there is a space between the ears
That must be filled, for better or for worse,
With wisdom, in the little span of years
That marks the way from go-cart to the hearse;
There is an element which men call time,
And who would seize it only grasps the tail,
And yet in passing flight it leaves behind
Its gob of precious wisdom in this vale :
And wisdom, Son, is what is taken home
To mark the point where whence divides from hence—
Time in itself can never fill the dome,
Future and past are but a change of tense;
Future and past are but before and after,
To mark the place where wisdom finds its mark—
And gripe and groan—so what!—or grin and laughter—
Wisdom divides the daylight from the dark.

"It's Kantian," says Marrowfat, "Neo-Kantian. The idea
of wisdom linked up with time as kind of a fifth dimension
is Kantian."

This, of course, is admitted. It certainly sounds a bit Kantian and more to the Author too. But Marrowfat does not
adduce any evidence that Grandfather Thurnow actually
wrote the poem. Grandfather Thurnow's influence is obvious.
He may have been addressing Jacob Binks, or talking to himself, which he was in the habit of doing, and Sarah may have

---

[1] *Ibid.*

taken it down and put it into verse, which she was also in the habit of doing. Or Sarah, with her amazing gift for projecting herself into her characters and speaking through them, may have been making a study of her grandfather that afternoon and speaking through him. With that splendid objectivity which distinguishes the real poet, she was able to lose her own personality and sometimes that of her readers in her characters, animate and inanimate, whose mood she seeks to interpret. In such lines as:

> I am Boreas, the North Wind
> I'm Violet, the flower, . . .

the reader will not be left in any doubt, and certainly in *Horse*, where the same reasoning may be applied as in the case of *Time*, even Marrowfat has not yet advanced the idea that Buttercup or any other of the Binks' horses was the real author. Let us examine the internal evidence of *Horse*, said by some [1] to be the finest delineation of horse psychology ever written.

HORSE

> Horse, I would conjecture
> Thoughts that spring in thee;
> Do, in contemplative hour,
> Teeming doubts thy soul devour,
> As in me?
> Does some yeasty cranial power,
> Intellectual force,
> Urge, in kindred doubts that grip us;
> "I, who once was eohippus,
> Now am horse;
> I have thinking,
> Therefore being,
> Therefore smelling,
> Feeling,
> Seeing;
> Therefore horse.
> Gloriously horse!

---

[1] "Plain horse sense," says the editor of the Detour *Herald*.

Horse I am but would be gladder
Could I see,
Evolutionary ladder's
Certainty;
Horse I am but can I know,
With the loss of final toe,
What to be?
Nought there is to tell me if
Pegasus or Hippogriff
Is destiny.
Oh well,
Horse's heaven,
Horse's hell,
Or super-horse,
Who can tell?
Who denotes?
What with knowledge and reflexes,
Self-expression and complexes,
Inhibitions and the sexes—
Give me oats.

Here the Binksian touch is at once apparent. Not only is there that keen and sympathetic understanding of animal psychology in which Sarah as well as her grandfather excelled, but the reference to the eohippus stamps the poem as peculiarly her own as plainly as the hall mark on silver. It is the geological motif again. But there is more direct evidence than this. When we examine the slightly damaged copy of Warden and Rockbuster's *First Steps in Geology* we find that the chapter devoted to evolution and paleontology contains an illustration of the eohippus itself. This picture shows the eohippus mounted on a rock and lost in the contemplation of a struggle to the death which is taking place at the base of the rock between a brontosaurus and a seal. But that it was the eohippus and the eohippus alone, which had caught and held Sarah's imagination is shown by the fact that its face has been modified, not altogether to its disadvantage, by the addition of a moustache and a pair of horn-rimmed spectacles. It is indeed fortunate for us that the copy of Warden and Rockbuster which so fortuitously fell into Sarah's hands was one of the first editions of this invaluable book. If it were not for this fact *Horse* might never have been written, or written differently. In the second and subsequent editions of Warden and Rockbuster the publishers have omitted the chapter on paleontology together with all references pertaining to the age of rocks in order to bring it into line with the Western School Act of 1931. But Fate definitely played into Sarah's hands here, and the result is *Horse*.

Professor Marrowfat's thesis becomes even more conjectural when we consider that great work entitled *Space*. Marrowfat maintains that *Space* was originally entitled *Beans*, and that Sarah merely changed the name and included it in her works. He maintains that when interpreted in this new light the internal evidence of *Beans* is at once apparent whereas that of *Space* is vague and uncertain. "I don't allow," says Marrowfat, "that Sarah could give advice about *beans*. I have had a lot of experience with women who cook beans and have never yet met one who could cook them properly. You might as well expect them to be able to fry a steak. I have made a study of food, more than that, I have made it a hobby. And this poem was written by a man."

There is something to be said for the point which Professor Marrowfat raises that the title of the poem has been changed. Sarah had been eating rather heartily that day and felt a bit unwell, and it is possible that she originally entitled the poem *Beans*. But we also know that she was working on a companion piece to *Time* at this period in order to round out the philosophical picture so beautifully begun in *Time* and completed in *Crisscrossers*. Moreover, as to the internal evidence, we know how masculine were the influences that acted upon Sarah, and when it came to beans she was, upon her own confession "a daughter of the Old South." [1] Marrowfat's contention that the poem could only be written by a man is therefore not based upon as wide an experience of women as he would have us believe. Beans were often the staple diet of the Binks household, especially during the last six or seven months of the winter, and Sarah was fond of them or starve. And that they produce wisdom, at time even visions, is well known. The fact that she put the words of wisdom into the

---

[1] Dakota.

mouth of Grandfather Thurnow apparently addressing Jacob Binks, or possibly Ole, is really Sarah addressing the world at large.

SPACE

The youth who satisfies with gruel
His carking appetite,
Will hunger more within the hour,
'Twill give him no respite;
But Wisdom set in straining jeans
Allays his urge on beans and buns;
For the ribs of he who lives on beans
Will never rattle when he runs;
The puling child may live on eggs,
But beans alone appease desire.
The youth who totters on his legs
Must learn this wisdom from his sire.

Sarah is here, with that splendid objectivity again which is the true mark of the artist, projecting herself into other personalities than herself and speaking through them. The same may be said of *Crisscrossers*.

CRISSCROSSERS

My son, if you should chance to meet
With him who walks with criss-cross feet,
Go mark him well, within that brain
Are seething thoughts that none can name;
    Go mark him well, and walk behind,
    His gait bespeaks the cosmic mind.

My son, such man along the street,
With glowing orbs and criss-cross feet,
Who breathes a great hilarity,
(Crisscrossers are a rarity),
    Has found in that cerebral ball
    The final meaning of it all.

My son, such man with mind aloof,
Is worth ten others on the hoof,
And he who walks with criss-cross gait
Can read the cosmos like a slate;
    Go mark him well with humble heart.
    Crisscrossers are a thing apart.

Never before had the Saskatchewan philosophy reached such heights or been so splendidly expressed. Even if Thadeus T. Thurnow had written this poem, as Professor Marrowfat contends, it would still stand as a monument. To read the cosmos like a slate! Sarah sets us the philosophical ideal in language which all can understand. That she received much of this ideal from Grandfather Thurnow, Old Sage, is all the more to her credit. For, that she did receive it, no one will deny. We know that Grandfather Thurnow was himself a crisscrosser on more than one occasion. His deep probings into the theory of the state, and his interest in politics in general tended to heighten this talent. Invariably on election night, in fact generally after a political discussion he prac- tised the crisscross on his way home from town. He was no bigoted partisan, as we have seen, both political parties were able to stimulate his massive mind to the same extent. Even Ole, inspired by his example, made attempts to achieve the "cosmic mind", but was never truly successful. His fossil footprints on the alkali flats show that Ole's path tended to cross and re-cross, but the gait itself is wide open, which is far from the perfection of the true crisscross which Sarah had in mind when she describes her grandfather. Moreover Ole tended towards mental fatigue on such occasions and Jacob Binks' "The dam' Swede's paralysed again", seems to indicate that he fatigued easily.

Professor Marrowfat, in his discussion of *The Prekantian and the Precambrian* suggests various sources from which Grandfather Thurnow may have acquired his philosophy, but he adduces no direct evidence that Grandfather Thurnow ever read the books mentioned, in fact, he adduces no direct evidence that Grandfather could read at all. This is a serious weakness in his argument. Moreover, there is very direct and conclusive evidence that even though Grandfather Thurnow might have been able to read, he was at least unable to write. This is shown by two facts: in one of her letters to

Mathilda, Sarah adds in a printed postscript, "Old Sage sends his love." Now it is exceedingly unlikely that he would have sent through a third person a message so intimate if he were able to pen it with his own hand. He himself stated on more than one occasion his opinion of Mathilda as being "not fit to print". But the final and conclusive proof that Thadeus T. Thurnow could not write has been unearthed by the Author with the assistance of the stenographer in the Land Titles Office at Quagmire, Saskatchewan. Exhaustive researches in the vault at the office have shown that *all three* mortgages pertaining to the N.E. Quarter of Section 37, Township 21, Range 9, West, are signed by Thadeus T. Thurnow with an X.

It is at once obvious that if Grandfather Thurnow could not write, he could not have written *Space*, and *Time*, and in fact, all those poems on which Professor Marrowfat bases his argument. It is gratifying that these brilliant researches of the Author have vindicated Sarah in the eyes of the Saskatchewan world, and that the shadow of the Binks-Thurnow controversy should be erased for all time. The ringing words of Principal Pinhole, "To deny the authenticity of these poems is to deny Sarah's genius", words which that savant has offered to repeat, if his expenses are paid, "from any rostrum in the country", will now ring endlessly.

7

Henry Welkin

THE YEAR 1926 marks the turning point in the hitherto un-eventful life of Sarah Binks. In spite of her growing fame she had remained a simple and unspoiled country girl, but now she was to make her first contact with the great outside world. She took a trip to Regina.

Regina marks a definite break in Sarah's career; all her later work was profoundly affected by it. "It is from this trip that we may definitely date the great change which came over all her poems; it is as if from that moment she put aside childish things forever and blossomed forth into the woman she gave promise of being even as early as her birth".[1] But the change was not effected without great trial. From Willows to Regina is a big step, in her case it was to prove almost too big a step. She was overwhelmed, and for a while the voice of the Sweet Songstress is stilled. One hesi-tates to think of Sarah had she been taken as far as Winni-peg, and one shudders to think of her in Toronto. But the Regina which overwhelmed her with its vastness and con-fused her with its throngs was at the same time the Regina which gave her something which she had never had, and which was to lead her eventually to one of the highest awards which has ever been bestowed upon one of Saskatche-wan's daughters, the Wheat Pool Medal.

Regina was at that time the Athens of Saskatchewan. At once the commercial as well as the literary and cultural centre of the province, it displayed a sophistication utterly alien to the mind of the untried country girl. Sarah's re-

---

[1] Rosalind Drool—*"Great Lives and Great Loves"*—Bunny-books Ltd.

actions were inevitable and might have been predicted; she felt crushed, inferior, her simple message lost in Regina's glitter, its allure. Fortunate indeed for the course of literature that Henry Welkin stood at her side in this hour, directed her thoughts, and showed her the real Regina behind its polish, its sophistication and its long rows of box cars.

Literature owes much to Henry Welkin; it must forever stand to his credit that it was through his influence that Sarah was brought into contact with the great world of commerce and culture. Had it not been for his generosity in paying all her expenses to Regina, Sarah might never have left Willows, and consequently her poetry might never have reached its maturity. Even though the sudden change from the pastoral simplicity of Willows to the teeming marts of men brought about that crisis in Sarah's life, her "Dark Hour", and threatened for a while to extinguish the divine spark and leave her forever dumb, we would not have it otherwise. "The bed on which the poet sleeps," says Sarah in one of her poems "is not always a bed of roses". What then shall we say for a poetess like Sarah herself?

Henry Welkin, aesthete, patron of the arts and letters, and travelling salesman, has been described as a man of considerable personal charm. He was tall and his eyes, which were set closely together, and appeared even more so from his habit of intense mental concentration, gave him an appearance of thoughtfulness and dignity. He was a careful and discriminating dresser; on the occasion of his first meeting with Sarah he wore a suit of brown striped serge, tailored according to the fashion of the day with long sweeping lapels, fancy pockets with buttons, the coat tight at the waist, and the trousers of the style known as "peg" ending in a four-inch cuff. A collar of the very best quality celluloid, a green bow tie, and a mauve silk shirt worn without a vest the better to display its full richness, and high-toed button shoes to match the suit completed the costume. Evidently a man of taste and discernment.

In spite of his success as a travelling salesman, Henry Welkin was not a man of action. His disposition tended to be retiring, as is shown by the remark of one of his contemporaries in the drug store: "Hank sure hates himself." On the other hand, as a travelling salesman, he had acquired from much travel a certain urbanity and carried himself with an air. He was not unpopular; the maids at the Commercial House invariably fluttered upon his arrival. Moreover at Charlie Wong's Snooker Academy his athletic prowess was recognized, and he was able to win from the youth of Willows no less (nor more) than their unstinted admiration.

Henry Welkin was skilled, perhaps too skilled, in the pen. He was not like Sarah a great artist, in that he lacked the articulateness of the artist, but he had made great strides in the struggle for self-expression. His flow of language could be at once picturesque and vigorous, and although he could never be called a poet in his own right, he collected sagas and folk songs and is known to have added verses to some of the older ballads like *Have You Heard of Lil'*. He was therefore quick to discern the possibilities of Sarah's genius, her charm of expression, and the unstudied simplicity of her thought.

The meeting of Sarah Binks and Henry Welkin took place in the Willows General store. The elder Binks, always a keen business man, had been holding his eggs for a rise, and had sent Sarah to town to enquire the price. She had, apparently, no other errands, or purchases to make if we except the usual pound of gum-drops for Grandfather Thurnow or the packet of snuff for Ole. Her mind, for once free of the long list of groceries, condition powders and insecticides, was therefore in that receptive condition which marks Sarah at her best. She felt, as she later related to Mathilda, "a poem coming on". And when the figure of Henry Welkin, who had followed her across the street from Charlie Wong's crossed her vision, she experienced at once that quickening of the spirit and that emotional response whereby the great have always recognized the great. No introductions were necessary; Henry Welkin, speaking with a confidence born of some inner feeling, said simply, "Hello Babe." Conventional words! Meaningless, or almost meaningless from a thousand repetitions! But the soul of the poetess leaped into perfect understanding. That same evening Henry Welkin called at Sarah's home and two days later sold Jacob Binks another tooth-harrow.

There are those who would see in the quick ripening of the friendship between Sarah Binks and Henry Welkin, something more than the spiritual and intellectual coming together of two kindred souls. Miss Rosalind Drool, in particular, has developed this theme in her recent book, *Great Lives and Great Loves* in which she dwells at some considerable length on the possibility, and, in fact, probability of a romantic attachment having sprung up between the two. Something may be said for this point of view. Making due allowances for Miss Drool's tendency towards over-emphasis, and her natural proclivity to take a vicarious and Freudian delight in incidents and experiences which she has not been privileged to enjoy, one may still admit that it would have been unnatural if these two, Henry Welkin and Sarah Binks, had not found in each other's personality some expression of their poetic faith. Sarah was never beautiful as beauty is counted, nevertheless, as Miss Drool repeatedly points out, she was by no means unattractive. She weighed at this time a hundred and thirty-four pounds, and her hair had been bleached by the Saskatchewan sun until it could almost be classified as blonde. Both eyes were blue, and her sensitive mouth revealed the winsomeness of her nature as well as the strength of her character. She was something of a hoyden, as who would not be under Ole's companionship, and felt most at ease when clothed in overalls and sweater, a costume which suited her personality in that here also she revealed the same grace and perfection of line which characterized her poetry.

We have seen that Henry Welkin, too, was not without that indefinable something. He may have appeared in Sarah's susceptible eyes a more glamorous figure than he actually was—certainly he shines more in the light of Sarah's effulgence than at Charlie Wong's—but he had youth and poise, and above all he brought to the young poetess something of the outside world. Moreover he knew farm machinery as few know their farm machinery. It would have been odd indeed if these two in their community of interests had failed to find at the same time a warm personal friendship. But it must always be emphasized that their chief interest lay in the world of art. The Author cannot stress this point too strongly.

It was during the interval between their meeting and the trip to Regina that Sarah wrote *Me and My Love and Me*. She had ample time to write. Henry was engaged in selling the elder Binks several more tooth-harrows, of which the farm already had a surplus but which both Jacob Binks and Ole loved to have around the yard and in the various fields. But it was not a period of great literary activity for Sarah. Only two poems have come down to us from this interval, but these two must be counted among the finest, not only of Saskatchewan, but of the whole of western Canada. In *Me and My Love and Me*, Sarah expresses in tones at once lyrical and subdued, her inner harmony with life.

ME AND MY LOVE AND ME

Over the moor at dusk there fled
    The dismal clouds, and we,
Facing the rain, with might and main,
    Me and my love and me.

The sea-gull screamed, the reeds were bent,
    But hand-in-hand the three,
We hurried on—going against wind,
    Me and my love and me.

There is a gentle strain of melancholy running through this poem which has led Sir Gelding Blitherstrip to compare her to the Russians, especially to Pupkin. But the comparison is rather far-fetched. Whereas Pupkin's melancholy arises from his unfortunate habit of drinking a mixture of wood alcohol and turpentine, Sarah's melancholy is one of joyous resignation. One need only read the other poem of this period to realize that Sarah's melancholy is neither the *Kwas* of the Russians nor the *Weltschmertz* of the Germans. Perhaps it is the *joie de vivre* of the French. In any case all great poetry is international. In *The Song of the Chore*, too well known to be quoted in full, Sarah rises on splendid wings and undoubtedly sets a new all-time record for lyrical height.

THE SONG OF THE CHORE

I sing the song of the simple chore,
Of quitting the downy bed at four,
And chipping ice from the stable door—
    Of the simple chore I sing :
To the forty below at break of day,
To climbing up, and throwing down hay,
To cleaning out and carting away,
    A paean of praise I bring.

Oh, it's time to milk or it's time to not,
Oh, it's time for breakfast and time I got
The pot of coffee in the coffee pot—
    I sing of the chore, "Hurray"!
Oh, it's time for this and it's time for that,
For mending unending and tending the brat,
And it's time to turn in and put out the cat,
    Tomorrow's another day.

Thus the Sweet Songstress in her hour of happiness. But Sarah was not to sing again for many a long day; her joy, her exuberance, her delight in the simple things, in Rover, in Ole, in the perennial calf, all were swept away in the rush of events which followed.

We do not know for certain how long Sarah spent in Regina. Professor Marrowfat, who for once treats Sarah sympathetically, even enthusiastically, limits the period to two and a half weeks. Doctor Taj Mahal, always a stickler for exactitude, has made a careful study of the railroad time tables of that period, and comes to the conclusion that the visit could not have lasted over a week, whereas Miss Rosalind Drool stretches it out to a full three weeks. Taking into account the personal error to which even the most careful investigators are subject, we may safely conclude that two weeks represent the length of Sarah's visit. But what crowded weeks! In that interval Sarah and Henry Welkin visited all the places of interest. Twice they went to the opera. Again and again they rode on Regina's street car. The cafés, China-town, the Botanical Gardens, the Union station—Henry Welkin was eager that his young *protégée* should drink life to the full. He took her to the aquarium and to the public library, and together they studied what fish and what manuscripts were available at these places. They made the rounds of the art galleries; they visited the parliament building and studied its geology. Nor was the world of commerce neglected; together they visited the department stores, the groceterias, the banks, the freight yards, and the big implement warehouse of the firm which Henry represented and which he was particularly anxious for her to see. Sarah drank it all in. She was eager and she had youth. But human nature, and especially a nature so human as Sarah's can encompass only so much. From Willows to Regina was a far bigger step than she had anticipated.

It may be that Henry Welkin erred in judgement in showing her so much in so short a time. Had he not gone so fast and so far the history of literature in Saskatchewan might have been different, not so rich, perhaps, nor so deep, but different. Already the inevitable reaction was setting in for Sarah. She was growing tired, one might almost say irritable. Certainly her reaction to Wascana Lake as a "mean little puddle; I could spit across it", is not the reaction of the Sarah we know to the great works of nature, and on the occasion of their visit to the implement warehouse on the afternoon of Thanksgiving Day it is believed that she was saddened by the sight of so much farm machinery under a roof. She hints as much in one of her letters to Mathilda, but also adds with some of her old-time recklessness and spirit, ". . . I'm danged if it wasn't interesting."

The visit was drawing to a close. Henry Welkin, probably inspired more than usual by the presence of the young authoress, decided upon some creative work of his own and took to the pen. Some confusion exists here as to the exact use of the terms "took to the pen" and "was took", terms which Sarah so often with careless indifference to the active and passive, uses interchangeably in her letters. Marrowfat understands the term "was took" to mean that Sarah's influence was so great upon Henry Welkin that he was no longer able to resist the urge to write; "in using the passive mood," says Marrowfat, "Sarah was undoubtedly expressing her own at the same time. Sarah herself must have often been aware of some inner necessity."

Took, or was took, Sarah returned to the farm and literature was thrown for a loss of many yards. It is difficult to form a correct judgement of Henry Welkin and the part he played in Sarah's life. Mr Justice Linseed, who recalls him in his book, *Eighty Years on the Bench*, speaks of him as a man of diversified talents, and adds, ". . . had he employed his great gifts in public life, he might have become Premier, or at least Leader of the Opposition."

8

The Dark Hour

REGINA HAD BEEN too much for Sarah. She went into a literary decline which lasted for months and from which even her nearest friends seemed unable to arouse her. It marks a sharp line between the two periods of her work which scholars generally refer to as Pre-Regina, and Post-Regina, or more simply, P. R. and P. R., respectively. Sarah herself refers to this period between the two P. R. periods as "My Dark Hour." For a while she wrote nothing, and where she writes at all she strikes the pessimistic note, sometimes even the macabre. What shall one say of *They Arose*, or *I Buried My Love at Dawn*, or even of *High on a Cliff*? There is something not entirely Saskatchewan in these verses, and the fragment,

> With grief engraven on my soul,
> I cannot roll in glee,
> The robin's note is but a dirge,
> The biscuit-bird grits me.

touches the subsoil of human depression. "It is more than her Dark Hour," cries Principal Pinhole in despairing tones, "it is Darkest Africa."

It is no mere coincidence that the manuscript of *Take Me Away* should be stained with tears, or what appears to be tears, and although later chemical analysis showed these to be butter and rhubarb jam, it does not alter the fact that in this period was her darkest moment. In *Take Me Away* she resists life's strongest appeal—that of food:

TAKE ME AWAY

Take me away, my eyes are red with weeping,
Leave me alone, I cannot, cannot stay;
Though you may offer these many things for eating,
        Take me away.

Take me away, I feel I must be going,
Hold me not back, I will not brook delay,
See, look, my red-rimmed eyes are glowing,
        Take me away.

Take me away, in vain this voice appealing,
I'll not remain; in vain I hear you say,
"It's early yet," my footsteps outward stealing,
        Take me away.

Sarah descends to her darkest in that trilogy (Sarah was fond of trilogies) *They Arose*, *I Buried My Love at Dawn*, and *High on a Cliff*.

THEY AROSE

They arose, three dead men,
Stiff and dank,
From the gloomy depths
Of a water tank;
And they bowed full soon
To the rising moon,
For the one was Bill,
And the other two, Hank.

I BURIED MY LOVE AT DAWN

I buried my Love at dawn,
And the bleak November wind,
Wailed low, "He is gone, he is gone,"
And the crow on the skeleton bough,
Croaked, "He is gone, he is gone!"
Alone on the heath I buried him,
My Love, my Soul—and the song
Of the wind and the crow still rings in my heart,
Tolls like a distant bell in my heart;
"He is gone, he is gone, he is gone!"

HIGH ON A CLIFF

High on a cliff of jasper and of quartz,
I sate at noon and looked upon the sea,
And gazed with leaden eyes upon my Love,
Drifting beyond this seeming world and me,
My Love, in pinchback coat and new plug hat,
Drifting upon an amber glowing sea;
And glowing too, in the noonday sun,
Three fountain pens, where the ripples run,
A trick cigarette case and a package of gum;
With leaden eyes I watched my Love drift by,
And watched the ripples blending with the sky.

It is not Sarah at her absolute best. But on the other hand, it is not Sarah at her absolute worst; and no matter how deep her depression, she never forgets her geology.

There are times, as in that classic lyric, *To a Star*, when Sarah seems to fall into a spirit of resignation:

TO A STAR

Methought I heard the tinkling of a star,
My heart did wilt within, and wiltering weeped,
And snivelling tears did splash the little stones,
And muffled sobs did make, and sobbing peeped.

With red-rimmed eyes, and through this moist,
    damp weep,
I glanced aloft, and hush, no more descried,
The tinkling star, its tinkling it had ceased,
Resoundingly I blew my nose and sighed.

But she falls again into utter depression with *Father, Thy Beard*:

FATHER, THY BEARD

"Father, thy beard no longer points,
Thy voice has lost its shrill!"
"My son, I quake within the joints,
Good luck hath turned to ill."

"Father, thy face is turning green,
Thou lookest like the hell!"
"My son, the things are what they seem,
Good luck hath sound its knell;
Yon pip-bird that we saw this morn,
Presages monetary clash,
And soon they'll take our hard-wrought corn,
Convert it into cash;
They'll take the hard-wrought corn and leave
Us nothing but the shortage,
They'll strip the cows, unbell the beeves,
To meet the chattel mortgage."
"Oh father, father, we must fly,
Oh father, we must out!"
"My son, here's mud into your eye,
My joints predict a drought."

Here at least Sarah speaks again with the voice of the
people, sad as she is, and there is a ray of hope in the last
two lines, but she falls again into that gloomy reverie with
those sad stanzas beginning

Come crush, harsh world, and snuff this life,
And bid my sorrows cease,
Rejected and dejected I
But long for my decease:

as well as in the fragment

When I'm buried in a graveyard,
And this feeble flame is snuffed,
Will a spotted magpie murmur,
Mutely sigh with ruff unfluffed?

Sarah is not only deeply despondent but seems to be
suffering from a bad cold in the head.

To cap Sarah's misery it was at this time that Rover
died. He had been complaining for some days of shortness
of breath, but appeared to be otherwise in good health; certainly no one suspected that the end was so near. He was
only sixteen years of age, and appeared to be in the full
flush and power of his doghood. On Sunday morning he had

caught six gophers, and had made a journey to one of the neighbours' dogs to get a fresh supply of fleas, of which he was running short. That same afternoon he complained of feeling unwell and his temperature rose. By the following afternoon his end was near. It came peacefully and painlessly, and his last effort was to wag his tail. No stone or board marks his last resting place. Somewhere on the edge of the coulee, overlooking the gopher meadows, and the alkali flats, overlooking the boundless prairie and that endless horizon broken only by the four elevators of Willows, Rover sleeps his long sleep, awaiting, as Sarah so poignantly puts it, "the last bark." The gophers scamper across the grave, and the tumbleweed which he had so often chased across the hundred and sixty acres stirs restlessly above him.

Two poems appeared in successive numbers of the *Hitching Post*. They are unsigned—Sarah was not the kind to make capital from the death of a friend and companion—but the authorship is in no doubt. The one is very short and appeared in the In Memoriam column of the *Post* under the heading *Rover Binks*:

> I had a dog who danced and spun,
> Who spun and danced when he was young,
>   And when he breathed he whistled,
> For his heart was full of fun.
> But his breath was coloured ash-grey,
> For he had an ash-grey lung;
>   Death struck him down in the afternoon;
> Henceforth my heart is filled with gloom.

In the other and longer poem entitled *Hymn to Rover*, Sarah expresses her longing and her hope.

HYMN TO ROVER

> When on that day the last bark rings
> To call the dog-like throng,
> Rover shall rise and don his wings,
> And raise his voice in song;
>   He'll raise his voice in song and sing,
>   In ecstasy of dog-like things.

And weaving patterns with their tails,
The joyous dog-like hosts,
Will lead him through celestial vales,
And miles and miles of posts,
    To meadows full of gopher holes,
      Which he can sniff and dig for moles.

Then shall I shout and throw a stick,
And bounce his ball and hide his bone,
Or stop and help him find his tick,
And call him to his home;
    His home where he can take his ease,
      In sunny spots and scratch his fleas.

And I shall take him by the hand,
And feed him mush, and pull his ears,
And he will grin, and understand,
And lick away these tears.
    On that great day of the final bark,
      Rover (as usual) will beat the lark.

There is a fine singing quality to these lines worthy of
Rover himself, and it has been set to music. It was sung at
the last Binks Festival at Willows by the massed choirs of
Quagmire, Pelvis, Detour, Hitching, Quorum, Baal, Vigil, Oak
Bluff, and Cactus Lake, and it was only due to the indisposi-
tion of the massed choirs of Eraser, Bentrib, Scandal, Album-
Junction, Jitters, and Dugout City, who had to pass the
Welcoming Committee of the Festival and receive their
badges at the Commercial House, that they were unable to
join in the rendering of this great song.

Between Rover and Regina life was almost too much for
Sarah. At times there is a ray of hope:

Perhaps some day I'll twang the harp,
And smite the lute with joyful sound;
Beribboned and bedecked in gay,
I'll ride around and 'round.

but her heart falters in the second verse and she falls again
into her gloomy reveries:

> But then perhaps in unknown grave,
> By burdock blown and boot betrod,
> I'll lie a full seven and a half feet deep,
> And push the daisies through the sod,

Even her lines do not quite scan, although some maintain that with the art that conceals art Sarah has deliberately introduced into the second from the last line the extra half dactyl in order to emphasize the extra half foot. Miss Diana Baby-Bunting, the literary critic of London, *Over the Tea Pot*, describes it as "Exquisite, exquisite."

Like all writers whose hearts are bruised, Sarah finally found refuge in nature. Nature and hard work are always the panaceas for the aching heart. Perhaps the last of the poems to come out of her Darkest Africa is *Death and Taxes*, but even here she is once more very near to the great heart of Saskatchewan:

> The grizzly Reaper with his scythe,
> Will never fail to take his tithe;
> And none there are within this life,
> Can ever dodge the Reaper's knife;
> The sticky infant in his crib,
> Or aged sire behind his bib,
> Or youth who dashes off to town,
> Are one and all cut down, cut down.
>
> Ah, some there are who have the luck,
> To last a while and run amuck,
> Or spend their time in simple play
> With simple maidens in the hay;
> But king and colonel, dude and duke,
> Alike are bundled in the stook,
> And one and all they pay his tax,
> And fall beneath the Reaper's axe.

It is an old theme, but Sarah puts new life into it.

During all this time Sarah had been doing very little work. Ole had helped her with the chores, and she had ample time to write. But now the spreading season, always one of the busiest on the farm, was at hand. Just as previously in *The Song of the Chore* she had hymned the praises of hard work,

so now she takes refuge in the labours of the farm. Hearken
to Sarah in that sweetly plaintive little lyric, *I Have No Time*:

> I have no time to write a line,
> No hour to pipe sweet lay,
> > No urge to shout,
> > Or muse roust out,
> The pitchfork calls away.
>
> I have no time to hunt for rhyme,
> No moments for delay,
> > The hand that wrote
> > Must grasp the spoke,
> And earn its chuck today.

The stern voice of duty called Sarah back to work, but
it repaid her in more than merely "earning her chuck today."
It gave her renewed hope and confidence and vigour, and she
forgets Regina in her joy in being once more at home within
as she expresses it in *Spreading Time*, "my own paternal field
and fold." In *Spreading Time* Sarah is once more herself, and
if she has any misgivings about the coming winter she dis-
misses them with the thoughts of spring.

SPREADING TIME

> It's joy again, for spreading time has found me,
> Within my own paternal field and fold,
> It's spreading time, and once more all around me,
> The air is rich, and fields are flecked with gold;
> From yonder heap the busy sparrow flutters,
> To other heaps, and all the heaps surveys;
> And from the dump the barnyard chicken mutters,
> And rooster lifts his solemn voice in praise.
>
> Alas, that winter's heavy cloak should ever
> Enfold this scene in dreary white, and bring
> The golden spots that mark our high endeavour,
> Beneath its blighted snow banks until spring :
> But spring will come, and what today we harrow,
> Will reappear, for spring makes all things new,
> The shovel and the stone-boat and the barrow,
> And what we spread will once more come to view.

It is evident that Sarah is once more finding herself. "It's joy again!" cries Sarah, and joy, sheer exuberance of joy is expressed in that paean of praise to the hunt, *The Duck Hunt*.

THE DUCK HUNT

The duck hunt, the duck hunt,
Ahoy, for the duck hunt,
Yahoo, the duck hunt so fine;
With my shot gun and duck-dog,
I'm off for the duck-bog,
And I leave for the duck hunt,
While yet there is time;
My loved one is weeping,
And clings to my side;
"Oh stay with me Oscar,
The duck hunt can ride,
Remain with me Oscar,
And let the duck hunt slide."
But hark, in the gloaming,
The moor-hens are moaning,
The marshes are sighing,
The sea gulls are groaning,
So I'm off for the duck hunt,
The duck hunt, the duck hunt,
I'm off for the duck hunt,
While yet in my prime.

It is Sarah at her absolute best. Even the much quoted *Jump into a Pleated Shirt*, does not quite equal it in its joyous abandon and vigour. In the latter she is more the observing and contemplative naturalist, and fails to reach the fine poetic frenzy which distinguishes *The Duck Hunt*.

JUMP INTO A PLEATED SHIRT

Jump into a pleated shirt friend,
And hurry with me away,
We'll visit the halleluiah bird,
That ushers in the day.

I'll show you where she lives, friend,
I'll show you what she eats,
And what she lays, so hurry, friend,
Jump into a shirt with pleats.

Her tail feathers are crimson, friend,
Her face is red with glee,
So into a pleated shirt, friend,
And hurry away with me.

I'll show you where she hides her young,
And covers them with dirt,
So hurry, hurry, hurry, friend,
Jump into a pleated shirt.

Professor Breather of St Midget's, in his series of radio talks, *The Sex Life of the Domestic Duck*, quotes this poem of Sarah's in corroboration of some observations he himself has made in Tahiti.

It is evident that Nature was taking Sarah by the hand. She wrote in quick succession *The Sparrow*, *By the Sycamore Tree*, and *Ode to the South-West Wind*, and a sonnet in Norwegian dialect, *To Ole*. These works of nature she treats with a simplicity and sympathy which she has never excelled. It is as if her trip to Regina and her Darkest Africa which followed had given her a new understanding. It is true, as Professor Marrowfat points out, that in the sonnet to Ole her knowledge of the Norwegian dialect is faulty, and that it might be equally well applied to Steve Grizzlykick, who boasted that his grandmother on his mother's side had fought at the Battle of Bonnington Falls and was thus over half Doukhobor, but it does not detract from the quality of Sarah's poesy. She was always weak in languages, as we have seen, but her poetry and her geology are sound. In *The Sparrow* we find again that sweet simplicity, and that oneness with nature which is the breath and soul of Saskatchewan literature.

THE SPARROW

A simple sparrow by the glen,
Despised by the best of men,
May help us greatly now and then,
    As we shall see.

A sparrow wandered o'er the hill,
O'er shingle, flat, and shiny rill,
To find some food, and eat his fill,
    Of little bugs.

He chanced upon a warty toad,
Who, toiling on the dusty road,
Did sweat beneath his heavy load,
    And cursed aloud.

The sparrow's face did beam with love,
Like dew beneath or stars above,
He got behind the toad and shoved,
    And moved the toad.

The warty toad was moved to tears,
Accustomed in declining years,
To nothing else but kicks and sneers,
    He thanked the sparrow.

What like unto this little song,
Where one doth help the other along,
Can make us great and keep us strong,
    I do not know.

It is a poem which has always had a peculiar appeal to Sarah Binks's feminine admirers, if any. Miss Rosalind Drool and Miss Diana Baby-Bunting, from widely separated parts of the Empire, unite here in describing it as "Exquisite, exquisite!"

With the sonnet *To Ole*, Sarah seems to have exhausted nature for the time being. Having found herself again and intact, she returns to those deeply reflective and full of hope poems which have so endeared her to her public. She scoffs at her own previous trepidations in *How Prone Is Man*.

HOW PRONE IS MAN

How prone is piebald man to mourn,
And make ado of nothing much,
To strew his rosy path with thorn,
And rusty nails, yea, plenty such.

Anon to quit his downy bed,
And greet the morn with drooping mush,
To scan with cross-eyed gleam in head,
The babbling birdlet on the bush.

With lowering brow he'll curse the cook,
And bid begone the hired man,
And gloomy thoughts are in his look,
And strife is written on his pan.

'Tis not for he the sparrow pipes,
Nor blows the bull-frog in the rill,
Ah, not for he the heron wipes,
His stately nose upon his quill.

Sarah wrote these lines, as she confessed to Mathilda, to reassure herself, but they might just as well have been dedicated to Jacob Binks. Certainly the Sarah who could write *The Duck Hunt* had no reason to have any misgivings as to her powers. That she did reassure herself is shown in that famous verse *Despond Not*, which breathes hope in every line.

DESPOND NOT

Despond not, though times be bale,
    And baleful be,
Though winds blow stout, a hurricale,
What's that, what's that to you and me.

Despond not, though frenzied fear,
    And pale-like hue,
May whisper panic in the ear,
What's that, what's that to me and you.

Despond not, for shame such speak,
　Aloft! Aloft!
Tut! Whistle low, with peakered beak,
　Soft, soft! Despond not!

Despond Not was published in Sarah's favourite organ,
The Horsebreeder's Gazette. The reception accorded it was
like that of *Spring*. It appeared at the psychological moment
when literature in Saskatchewan was at one of its low ebbs.
It had been a drought year and edition after edition of *The
Horsebreeder's Gazette* had appeared without a single line
of poetry. The appearance of *Despond Not* followed almost
immediately by a heavy rain touched the almost forgotten
chords in the hearts of the people. "Despond not!" cried
Sarah Binks, and "Despond not!" echoed Saskatchewan. She
had arrived. Never again would Sarah have to sell subscriptions in order to have her works see the light of print. Henceforth the literary journals of Saskatchewan were thrown
open to her free of charge.

"Despond not!" cried the Hon. A. E. Windheaver at the
unveiling of Sarah's monument, "Despond not! I give you
the words of your own great poetess, than whom there is no
greater in this great Province of which I have the honour
to be Minister of Grasshopper Control and Foreign Affairs.
Despond not! Come drought, come rust, come high tariff and
high freight rates and high cost of binder twine, I still say
to you, as I have already said to the electors of Quagmire
and Pelvis, that a Province that can produce a poet like your
Sarah Binks under the type of government we have been
having during the last four years, full of graft and malad-
ministration and wasting the taxpayers' money, and what
about the roads, I want to say, that a Province that can produce such a poet may be down but it's never out."

9

Recognition and Success

LOOKING BACK OVER the years and comparing Sarah Binks's early struggle for recognition with the fame that she was later to achieve, it is difficult to understand why she remained so long in comparative obscurity. It is true that if her voice had never reached beyond Willows or if her message to the people of Saskatchewan had never extended beyond the barbed wire surrounding the North East Quarter of Section 37, Township 21, Range 9, West, she would still have written reams. But one hates to think of that pellucid stream of poesy soaked into the arid soil of the Binks' homestead. That soil might have been enriched thereby, but Saskatchewan as a whole would be poorer. And it is to the undying credit of the people of Saskatchewan that her genius should have been recognized during its flowering, and that they should have conferred upon her during her brief life some tangible evidence of the high regard in which her work was held. It is the tragedy, the great, ironic tragedy of Sarah Binks' life that this first tangible evidence of her success, the horse thermometer, should also have been the instrument of her death, the fatal dagger which stilled her voice forever. But it is a splendidly fitting tragedy. Sarah would not have had it otherwise. The McCohen and Meyers Stock Conditioner Company may well say, "If we had known that the horse thermometer was going to carry her off we would have given her instead a hypodermical needle of which we also carry a full line." But between a hypodermic needle and a horse thermometer, Sarah would have unhesitatingly chosen the horse thermometer. The will to live was strong in her, but the will to self-expression was greater. Always the poetess first, always conscious of her own great destiny, she realized that she would have to pay the price of greatness. Death loves a shining mark. The choice would have to be made, and in her having to make it may lie the true explanation of her former depression, Miss Rosalind Drool notwithstanding. It is true that much, if not most of it may be attributed to Regina, but Sarah could never have reached that high resolve without passing through Darkest Africa. She realized that her powers might fail and her courage falter:

> The finest flower I have known,
> The rarest blossom I have met,
> Has gone to seed, her beauty flown,
> Her day is done, her sun is set.

> "This makes me scratch myself and ask,
> "When shall my powers fade?"
> It puts me severely to the task,
> To face this fact undismayed.

"To face this fact undismayed!" Between a hypodermic needle and a horse thermometer, even if she had been aware of its fatal implications, Sarah would have chosen the horse thermometer.

The great literary contest sponsored by the McCohen and Meyers Stock Conditioner Company is history in the annals of the Quagmire Agricultural Society Fair. The exact conditions of the contest as originally outlined, have been preserved in the Binksian Collection whose trustees were fortunate enough to obtain a copy of *Swine and Kine*, where the announcement first appeared. Sarah herself was not a subscriber to *Swine and Kine*, and Jacob Binks, as a true dirt farmer, disdained it as a woman's magazine. "The dam' thing is all about pigs." But the self-contained economics of the Schwantzhacker menage *was* concerned with pigs and they regularly received a copy. Sarah was able to peruse it whenever the thirteen sisters had finished reading the advertisements and Mathilda was permitted to carry it across. The opportunity thus afforded the thirteen Schwantzhacker sisters to express themselves for Sarah's benefit in marginal comments and drawings proved to be a greater literary opportunity for her than for them. She seized at once upon the McCohen and Meyers' announcement, and so great was her preoccupation that she forgot, for once, to cross the eyes of all the illustrations of pigs and their owners in *Swine and Kine* before returning it to the thirteen sisters.

The epoch-making contest of the McCohen and Meyers Stock Conditioner Company was absolutely free. "Free! Free! Send no money! You too may win a prize!" must have been the words that first caught Sarah's attention. Saskatchewan owes much to the philanthropy of McCohen and Meyers. Their brilliant inspiration of improving both the stock and the literature of Saskatchewan in one contest, touching, as it does, both the soul and the material welfare of the people, has won them a place in every heart.

In the preamble to the terms of the contest the merits of the stock conditioner are set forth, and the earnest need of improving the stock as well as life on the farm in general is emphasized. The announcement of the award of a prize for the best poem dealing with some farm animal, together with the rules of the contest followed :

1. Send no money! This contest is absolutely free.
2. For the best poem dealing with stock or farm animals, a prize, together with a certificate, will be publicly awarded at the Quagmire Agricultural Fair, or any other Fair in the B Class which the successful candidate may elect.
3. All poems must be written on one side of the paper only.
4. All poems must be in English.
5. All poems must be the author's own work and must not have been published before.
6. Poems must not be too long. Remember merit counts. It is better to send a short good poem than a long bad one.
7. *Important!* Every entry must be accompanied by THREE labels from the packages of McCohen and Meyers Stock Conditioner, and must bear the signature and portait of Adolf McCohen, the discoverer of this great farm and home remedy.
8. You may submit more than one poem, in fact, it is advisable, because the more entries you make the greater your chances of winning a prize, but each

poem must be accompanied by THREE labels from McCohen and Meyers Stock Conditioner, and must bear the signature and portrait of Adolf McCohen, the discoverer.

9. In the event of a tie, or if two or more contestants submit the same poem, the award will be made on the basis of neatness and spelling.

10. The award of the judges is final. This is positive.

11. All entries must be in the hands of the Contest Editors on or before the closing dates as announced.

12. The successful candidates must pay their own ex penses to and from the Fair grounds, but arrangements will be made to give them an exhibitor's badge which will entitle them to free entry into the grounds.

Address all entries to McCohen and Meyers Stock Con ditioner and Supply Company, 1629½ Park Lane, Regina, Saskatchewan.

Sarah's decision to enter this contest was immediate, but not without some misgivings. True, she could qualify on most counts; she was willing to comply with the regulations as set forth, to submit only her own work, to write on one side of the paper, in English, to abide by the decision of the judges, and to send no money. But she was anxious to submit at least two of her poems in the confident expectation that they would be tied for first place and that one of them would naturally be declared the winner on the ground of neatness if not spelling. Her quick imagination even dwelt upon the idea of a third and fourth entry, although no prizes were to be awarded for the place and show positions. But here her imagination outstripped practicality, for although Jacob Binks used the McCohen and Meyers Stock Conditioner for his horses, to induce him to buy a full twelve packages at one time was more than Sarah could expect. She might possibly, with Mathilda's assistance, persuade some of the more distant neighbours who might not themselves have literary aspira tions, to buy the stock conditioner, and undoubtedly her grandfather, if it were suggested to him, would incorporate it into the formula and mash of a new turnipin tonic on which he was working at the time. A reasonable supply of dis coverer McCohen's autographed portraits was thus assured, but the rate of consumption of the stock conditioner on the

Binks' farm would have to be increased to balance the literary output which Sarah had in mind. She was too much the daughter of Jacob Binks not to realize that an unbalanced economy would result in waste, and she therefore issued orders to Ole that the horses were to receive double their rations of condition powders for the time being and, as an afterthought, that he himself was to have some on his porridge every morning.

Time was to show, of course, that Sarah's plan, farsighted as it was, was successful even beyond her expectations. Not only, as we now know, did Sarah win a much coveted prize at the Quagmire Agricultural Fair, but so also did the Binks' horses. Three seconds and one honourable mention stand to their credit, and the ribbons of Buttercup and Dairy Queen are today among the most prized possessions in the collections of Binksiana. It was a big day for the Binks family. Old Sage's Tonic and Hair Remover created surprise and delight when it was tested by the judges and was placed in a special class. Even Ole, in splendid condition, won a box of cigars for repeatedly ringing, and finally breaking, the bell with the twenty pound mallet.

But these were events of the future. In the meantime Sarah devoted herself to the literary problem that lay before her, what poems to submit and what farm animals to choose. *Horse, Calf, The Goose, Steeds*, and *The Cursed Duck* had already been published and were therefore not eligible poems. True, she could write again on the same themes, but she felt that she had exhausted these subjects, or, as Jacob Binks expressed it, "ploughed, harrowed, and cross-harrowed." Her keen sense of literary values told her also that of all the manuscripts submitted in this competition, ninety-five per cent would undoubtedly deal with horse or cow and she recognized the value of originality in a competition of this kind. For a while she considered the indigenous gopher as a fitting farm animal, but in the end abandoned it as too trivial. As a fur-bearing animal it had some value in the tail, but its economic value had yet to be established. Mathilda's suggestion that the *Sonnet to Ole*, of which she was very fond, be submitted, was also ruled out. Sarah pointed out that the judges might not regard Ole as strictly speaking a farm animal, moreover, the Norwegian dialect, in which the sonnet was written, might disqualify it as not being strictly speaking English, and in any case it was too long. There remained, apparently, only the pig and the sheep, and because the pigs she knew were those associated with the Schwantzhacker farm, she was, as she herself confessed, "unable to treat them sympathetically." In fact, she had already expressed herself concerning them in one of her notes to the Schwantzhacker sisters;

> Of all the farmer's bird and beast,
> I think I like the pig the least.[1]

She therefore turned her attention to sheep.

PIGS

> The man who raises pigs for cash
> May leap for joy to give them mash,
> And laugh aloud to meditate
> The liver sausage on his plate,
> Transform the barley and the bean
> To strips of fat and strips of lean,
> And see all things, his barns and yard
> And wife and child in terms of lard.

---

[1] The complete manuscript of this hitherto unpublished poem has recently been discovered in the office files of *Swine and Kine* by Professor Mush, who has a nose for that sort of thing. It was sandwiched between two bundles marked "Rejected Manuscripts" and "Unpaid Subscriptions." It was also the place where the stenographer kept her lunch. This fortunate coincidence led Professor Mush to the discovery of the manuscript of *Pigs*, which had been given up for lost, but whose former existence had always been assumed. The manuscript by this time presents the appearance of a papyrus, and is badly stained, but whether this is due to Sarah's or to the stenographer's lunch has yet to be determined. Professor Mush is continuing his investigations by a study of the stenographer's eating and other habits, and in the meantime has sent a photostatic copy of the priceless manuscript to *Le Bureau Scientifique* for chemical analysis. The poem itself, can, however be deciphered. It evidently belongs to Sarah Binks P.R. period.

But such a man without his will,
Must pay the price in more than swill,
His mind may dwell on pig in death,
But his eyes are crossed from holding breath,
And he who follows where he goes,
Must wear a clothes-pin on his nose :
Of all the farmer's bird and beast,
I think I like the pig the least.

Sarah's experience with sheep had been limited to the portrait of the prize ram which hung in the parlour facing that of Thadeus T. Thurnow as a companion piece, and to the opinion of Jacob Binks that "where the dam' sheep have passed nothing ever grows". She attempted one poem based on the study of the portrait, but only got as far as a few lines:

THE PRIZE SHEEP

My son, yon sheep that gazes into space,
Conceals his thoughts behind yon sheep-like face,
For he who wins the prize must ever train
His features never to express disdain;
Who wins the ribbon or the laurel here,
Must never frown, or laugh from ear to ear,
But in his features, speech and all his acts,
Express profound acceptance of the facts.

But Sarah did not continue this poem. For one thing, it might be attributed to her grandfather, and for another it was too philosophical. Sarah was becoming a little weary of philosophy, for which no one can blame her. It is almost as if for the time being she steps out of character and becomes the least bit shrewish. It is not the most popular of all her poems and Professor Marrowfat might have made a better showing in the Binks-Thurnow controversy if he had analysed the internal evidence here instead of *Space, Time*, and *Crisscrossers*. But Sarah was dealing with a subject which was not only difficult in itself but was unfamiliar to her. She comes much closer to the great heart of Saskatchewan when she abandons her contemplation of the two portraits and lets her imagination go on *Hordes of Sheep*, the poem which she submitted, and which was tied for first place. In *Hordes of Sheep* she seems to confuse the sheep with the buffalo herds of Saskatchewan's early days, but unfamiliar as the subject must have been to her, the West, the country of the big open spaces, was not and the spirit of the West blows through every line of it. It was this which the judges must have had in mind when they gave it first place immediately on its receipt but later demoted it to second place, or tie, when Sarah's other entry appeared:

HORDES OF SHEEP

'Tis night on the prairie and night on the plain,
And all is still—no sign of rain—
And all is peace, and deep in his teepee
The red man sleeps and his squaw is sleepy;
The red man snores with the red man's cunning;
But hark, what's that? 'tis the sound of running,
'Tis the sound of rushing, of hurrying feet,
And hark, what's that? 'tis the sound of bleat;
Louder it comes, it rises wild,
Ah, the mother hears it and grabs her child,
Louder still, the frantic mother,
Grabs her child, and another and another;
And the red man waked by that hurrying tread,
Turns deadly pale beneath his red;
The Indian Brave is roused from sleep;
"Run for your life boys, here come sheep!"

A night of terror, the desolate dawn
Counts many a brave that was trampled on,
And nothing grows where the sheep have passed,
But, things that come must go at last;
And the years roll by, and it's once more night,
But where is that echoing tread of fright?
That thundering horde that swept like fire,
Is bits of wool on the barbed wire;
And the monarch has traded his high estate
For bed and board and the right to mate,
And gives his wool quite meek and mild,
To the red man's wife for her latest child;
And soundly the Brave, on his reservation,
Sleeps in his woollen combinations.

"Epic," cried the critics when it appeared, "simply epic!" Even Marrowfat, usually sober, rises to enthusiasm. "There is no doubt," he declares, "that Sarah wrote this one. I see no suggestion of the mature wisdom of Thadeus T. Thurnow here. The inspiration is Ole's, if any."

Sarah submitted *Hordes of Sheep* with every confidence. But her active mind, intent upon a second entry, at once began to cast about for another farm animal. The same difficulty which she had previously experienced presented itself, a shortage of farm animals. She did not like to venture into the field of poultry. "Poultry and poetry don't mix," she had once told Mathilda, and this in spite of the success of *The Cursed Duck*. It was therefore a fortunate day for her when the farm skunk whose home was in one of the farther reaches of the coulee, paid one of his infrequent visits to the Binks home and decided to stay over for the week-end. Here was Sarah's inspiration. She had completely forgotten about the skunk and her quick intuition told her at once that she would have a free field, in the matter of literary theme. Few farms in the dry belt were fortunate enough to have one of these quaint animals within their borders and were obliged to depend almost entirely on the pail-smudge to control their mosquitoes. But welcome as was the skunk, it resisted all attempts at domestication, preferring the free life, if hazardous at times, to the security of "bed and board and the right to mate," for which the once proud sheep had sold its heritage. Sarah admired the skunk for its independence, but also mildy resented its manner of resisting all advances, especially after Ole's friendly overtures had been met with a distant snub. With deft sureness she puts her finger on the one weak spot in the skunk character, its pride.

THE FARM SKUNK

I take it that the skunk is proud,
And uses devious device,
To hold himself aloof from crowd,
Surrounded himself with social ice.

He tends to give himself an air,
And has been known to snub his betters,
His attitude a bored hauteur,
Like those who talk of art and letters.

He lifts his eyebrows to his peers,
    Attempts at friendliness annoy him.
No wonder that in course of years
    His very best of friends avoid him.

Sarah polished and re-polished this poem and had Mathilda
check its metre before she submitted it to the contest editors.
It is a short poem, but she decided that under Rule 6 of the
contest it might stand a better chance than *Hordes of Sheep*
which was not so short. But short as it is, it has a brilliancy,
almost a sophistication which is unusual in her. Regina had
done something to Sarah. That Athens of Saskatchewan had
perhaps taught her more than Henry Welkin had anticipated.
The poetess who can use "bored hauteur" so casually has
come a long way from the Sweet Songstress of Saskatchewan
who wrote *Blade of Grass* and *The Parson's Patch*. True, the
mail order catalogues were employing more and more college
graduates to describe the feminine pages, and "hauteur" had
replaced "chic" in more than one edition, but Sarah was beginning to understand things that she had never understood
before. That grace and perfection of line which had always
distinguished her was becoming, if anything, more graceful.
It is not for nothing that she is sometimes known as The
Poet's Poetess. Certainly no one has ever excelled her in the
graceful tribute she pays to one of Saskatchewan's greatest
statesmen in those brief lines, *The Premier*, in which she casts
the Honourable Grafton Tabernackel in the role of that self-
sacrificing Roman, Cincinnatus, who left his oxen and plough
in the field when the call came to give his talents to the
state. Sarah expresses too the opinion widely held that the
Honourable Grafton Tabernackel had done his duty and
should receive his reward in greater leisure and time for his
hobbies.

THE PREMIER

He heard the call to service and arose
    At once, (his ear was tuned to just that pitch)
Left field and ox, nor stopped to change his clothes,
    Left plough and harrow idle in the ditch.

His ear was finely tuned to just that sound,
    Ah, well attuned—will someone tell us now,
What note will reach that ear pressed to the ground,
    And call back Cincinnatus to the plough.

Sarah wrote these lines while waiting for the announcement of the award and intended to recite them at the Quagmire Agricultural Society Fair, upon receiving the prize of whose nature she was still in ignorance but which she rightly surmised would have to do with farm animals. She hoped that it would not be an extra package of the stock conditioner. The horses were looking very well as it was, and Ole was very fit, in fact, Mathilda had complained that he was almost too fit and had suggested less cereal for breakfast.

The announcement of the award and the publication of *The Farm Skunk*, by Sarah Binks, of Willows, Saskatchewan, gave Sarah no surprise. She had expected it, and her only doubt had been whether *Hordes of Sheep*, or *The Farm Skunk* would be awarded first place. What was surprising, however, was the storm of protest which arose over the award, a storm which surprised even those hardened contest holders, Messrs McCohen and Meyers, themselves. That a comparatively unknown author, and a girl, should stir up such a tempest gave them cause for reflection. Not only were there protests from the disappointed contestants, they were accustomed to that, but that the protests should arrive from those who had neither participated in the contest nor used their stock conditioner, showed that they were dealing with a new star on the literary horizon. From a single farm near Willows, twelve separate letters had arrived protesting the award, chiefly on the grounds that Sarah Binks had lost her amateur standing and that she was not therefore eligible to compete in a contest of this kind which was obviously for non-professionals. The letters pointed to the publication of *Horse* and *Spring* as outstanding examples of her professional work. Other protests raised the technical objection that a skunk was not a farm animal within the meaning of the act or rules; others again accused the judges of favouritism and declared that Sarah had been given the first place entirely on the grounds of neatness and spelling, whereas others protested that the terms of the contest had been made too difficult and that the award should be made on the grounds of neatness and spelling only. To all objections, except those which went so far as to revile the portrait of Adolf McCohen on the packages of the stock conditioner, the judges duly replied, pointing out that nothing had been said as to the eligibility of professionals, that this was an open contest, that Sarah had been awarded no marks for neatness and spelling, and that she had complied with the rules. The most serious objection, namely, that the farm skunk was not a farm animal, they admitted as having some foundation. Their original intention was to regard as farm animals only those whose condition could be improved by their stock conditioners, but they had every confidence in their products and had no doubt that the skunk would feel much better and probably put on weight if their stock conditioner were given him. The judges admitted, however, that in reading Sarah's poem, they had misread "The Farm Skunk" as "The Farm Chunk", and that this variety of light draught horse very properly came under the Farm Animal Act of 1904. The chunk was as proud a horse as the skunk was proud a skunk, and the poem could be read in either way and make as good sense. In any case, under Rule 10 of the contest they were not permitted to change their decision, "This is positive." In his Memoirs [1] Adolf McCohen recalls, "I myself acted as judges because it was an important contest and Meyers counted the labels. We seen right away from the protests that this Sarah had something, and I said to my partner this girl is going to be a writer perhaps or in advertising and better keep an eye on her there might be a percentage in it. So we decided to give her one of our horse thermometers instead of the three-colour lithograph of Dan Patch which we generally give in contests of this kind not that they don't cost just about as much but it seemed to be attracting a lot of attention."

The big day of the Quagmire Agricultural Society Fair arrived soon after the announcement of the award. Sarah received her exhibitor's badge and was duly notified to be somewhere in the neighbourhood of the grandstand during the middle of the afternoon. The Hon. Grafton Tabernackel himself, who had opened the fair, consented to present the prize in person but was unfortunately engaged at the moment

---

[1] McCohen, A.—*Proceedings of Saskatchewan Bankruptcy Commission*, 1932.

in opening some special exhibits behind the sheep barn when Sarah's name was called. Her appearance when she stepped onto the platform was the signal for tumultuous applause. She had been preceded by a trapeze act and the next item on the list of attractions was to have been a symbolic dance by Lolita, one of the performers from the far end of the midway who had been brought to Quagmire at tremendous expense for this occasion. It was an exceptionally windy day and the grandstand had been looking forward to this act with much anticipation, especially after one of the trapeze artists had just been blown off the trapeze and had landed on the third base of the adjoining baseball diamond where a game was in progress, and from which position of vantage he was able to score for Quagmire. Sarah herself had some misgivings about the wind when she stepped onto the platform and her attention was occupied with it to such an extent that for some time she was mistaken for Lolita and given round after round of applause. In fact, it was not until Adolf McCohen, rising to the occasion in the absence of the premier, presented Sarah with the bright and shining horse thermometer, that the public was really aware that their new poetess had come among them. As Sarah shook Adolf McCohen's hand to receive his congratulations, the cheer which arose like a blast of wind, and almost simultaneously with it, showed how Saskatchewan had taken her to its great heart. She bowed her acknowledgements and recited that graceful tribute to the premier, but owing to the fact that the Quagmire band at that moment burst into its rendering of Red Wing, and to the fact that the Guernsey bull, Grand Champion Molloch II, decided to leave the judging ring for the ball game and score nine runs for Pelvis, Sarah's graceful tribute did not at that time receive the publicity it deserved.

Sarah's first act on returning home that evening was to destroy *Ode to the South-West Wind*. She may have felt, with her new honour and conscious of her responsibility as a public character, a feminine Laureate of Saskatchewan, that her work should be more critically scrutinized, and that none should go down to posterity without the hall mark of perfection. Whatever the reason, *Ode to the South-West Wind*, the first of a series or cycle of eight poems which she had planned and in which she had intended to box the compass so completely that nothing more need ever be written about the winds, was destroyed and the whole splendid conception of the cycle was abandoned. But it was to be replaced by a larger and more splendid conception. Those haunting lines

> Should maddened pterodactyl chance to meet
> With raging crocodile,
> Then crocodile the pterodactyl eat
> Or pterodactyl eat the crocodile.

were once more beginning to haunt her. That epic, that super-epic, *Up from the Magma and Back Again,* whose outlines she had vaguely sketched back in those days when William Greenglow had first opened for her the treasures of Warden and Rockbuster—and how long ago it all seemed—that epic was now to take form. Profoundly philosophical, profoundly geological, rich in soil and rock and the experiences of life, all of whose depths Sarah had plumbed, it was to lead her to Saskatchewan's highest honour and no less a person than the Hon. A. E. Windheaver was to pin the Wheat Pool Medal upon her breast.

Up from the Magma was not written in a day. A full winter was to pass and its heavy cloak was to "enfold . . . beneath its blighted snow-banks" the entire Binks' farm for many a long month before it was completed. Sarah was happy, profoundly, contentedly happy. The chores were light, the afternoons were long, and Jacob Binks had presented her one Christmas with almost a cubic foot of unused mortgage and auction-sale handbills which he had acquired from the Quagmire printery and upon whose backs Sarah could write and write. Ole chewed his cigars and Mathilda returned from the fair and managed to send word across to the Schwantzhacker farm that she would continue her visit with Sarah until the next chinook. Once a day the two girls took the temperature of all the Binks's horses with Sarah's thermometer, and once at least, Jacob Binks used it when Ole returned through a blizzard from a political meeting, "to see if the dam' Swede's as hot as he looks."

Alas, the horse thermometer. That fateful instrument which had so often taken the temperature of the horses and which had been the first step towards renown, and without whose encouragement *Up from the Magma* would never have been written, was to be the fateful cause of her untimely death. Happy Sarah, who could write with this sword of Damocles hanging over her. If she was aware of what lay in store for her she gave no sign. "To face this fact undismayed" was written upon her shield henceforth. If she had any premonition, her works during this final year do not show it. *The Magma* is full of hope, and the calm acceptance of life.

10

Up From the Magma

SARAH HATED WINTER. Time and again she had expressed her opinion of its heavy cloak, of its "blighted snowbanks" and their four-foot depths, and once at least, as we know from her letters to Mathilda, she had expressed all her opinions with consummate mastery in a final summation, "if it warent for the helldam snow." But for once also she faced the winter with fortitude and bravery;

> Beyond the dripping nose and tear,
> Beyond the chilblain and the bite,
> Beyond the scratchy underwere,
> Beyond the eighty-below at night,
> There still must lie—though drifts conceal—
> Some hidden good for man's descry,
> Some secret bounty for his weal,
> Which man should shovel out—or try.

Thus Sarah Binks begins her great epic, *Up from the Magma and Back Again, Canto I, The Great Ice Age.* And let this be said for Sarah; whatever her private opinion of that age may have been in terms of chilblains and scratchy "underwere", the inner eye of the poet looks always beyond these things for some hidden good. Moreover all effort carries with it its own reward even though it be only exercise. The virtuoso must always practise, and Sarah, the self-conscious possessor of a horse thermometer, and with a cubic foot of handbills in front of her, was now suddenly aware that winter, her usual fallow season, must also receive its share of effort. That hidden good, that secret bounty for man's weal, might or might not be there beneath the drifts. She would shovel it out—or at least try. And let this also be said for Sarah; she certainly shovelled it out.

It was not easy. Time and again Sarah would grow discouraged and the winter, after all, was long. And much of *Canto I, The Great Ice Age*, is taken up with the anticipation of *Canto II, The Great Spring Thaw*. Moreover the mechanical difficulties of her ambitious venture were by no means small, as anyone must know who has undertaken to write a cubic foot of verse. Often enough the burners grew dim in their lamps, and the cold would creep in as the fire in the Quebec heater died down to its single navigation light. No sound except her grandfather's rhythmic snore, and—from the anteroom—Ole's sneezes with which he regularly marked the hour and the half-hour in all his sleeping, would break the silence of that long prairie night. And Sarah, struggling into another overcoat and her grandfather's felt boots, would help herself to a plate of cold beans and go back for just one mcre rhyme, often enough, alas, only to echo the plaint of all poets from time immemorial;

> He knows not life, the one who never ever,
> Has burned the midnight coal-oil in his time,
> And donned two overcoats in stern endeavour,
> To wrestle with the spelling and the rhyme :
>   He knows it not, the anguish of the poet,
> Who never sat all night and cursed the pen,
> And writ a word, and rubbed out what he wroet,
> And once more wrote, and rubbed it out again :
>   Ah, what knows he of deep dyspeptic sorrow,
> Whose turning-in is blocked with poet's rage,
> And waits the word—until the dawn's cold morrow
> Sees only rubbed-out marks across the page.

Actually it is doubtful whether Sarah ever thus awaited the "dawn's cold morrow". Beans tended to make her sleepy among other things and as a rule she had turned in and was dead to the world by the time Ole had struck ten. But even this hour—countered to some extent by the beans—would lower her natural buoyancy the following day. Her art, then, becomes "a thin chimera", and she dwells upon the sadder aspects of writing, even to the extent of wondering whether

it might not get her down. With stern fortitude she accepts
the responsibilities of her calling;

> Let no one say, when I have reached my ending,
> The poet find his balsam of relief
> In only joy and laughter for life's mending,
> And never throws a passing glance at grief :
> Art may be nothing but a thin chimera,
> To get us down but still 'twere better said;
> "She wrote! Beneath this marble slab lies Sarah.
> A Poetess—and prematurely dead."
> For he whose brow would wear the jaunty laurel
> Must never let the lines of sorrow fade—
> Literature is mostly doleful choral,
> And grief the poet's steady stock in trade.

But it was never for long. The Sarah who had passed
through Darkest Africa, and had come out whole and with a
horse thermometer, could never again sink into real despond-
ency. "Give me a line to fling at fame", she cries with her
next breath, "that deals not with the woes of man". She
will have none of it, at least none of it as written upon man's
countenance, and least of all upon her own :

> Give me a line to fling at fame,
> That deals not with the woes of man,
> Whose troubles of the day and dame,
> Are writ in wrinkles on his pan;
> That furrowed story of his trials,
> And calendar of years on earth,
> May noble be—but give me dials
> That split from ear to ear in mirth.

> Each winter's frost-bite, and the bug
> That greets the spring will leave its mark,
> As well as sorrow on the mug
> Of infant, youth, and patriarch—
> But all those records of this vale,
> Of time, and life's ennobling grief,
> Embossed in Gothic or in Braille,
> I'd leave to others, just as lief.

All too little is known of *Up from the Magma and Back Again*. It has never yet been read in its entirety. Of the canto written in Mound-Builder only a few paragraphs are as yet available to the reader in English. Always a difficult language to translate, the work is proceeding slowly and with great caution so as not to lose the finer shades of meaning which Sarah Binks intended to convey. But already it is becoming increasingly apparent that Sarah, with the insight of genius, has called from Saskatchewan's historic past characters who speak to us across the years in words which never die. And from those living pages Vesuvius, the Mound Builder, steps forth, and his voice is the voice of Saskatchewan:

> My Friends! You have heard Afflatus. You have heard Afflatus say to you, "Come and be my friends. We will build mounds, and yet more mounds. There will be work for all!" Four years ago you heard Afflatus say these things. And again today. Has Afflatus built mounds? Yes. Some. But what mounds! My friends, there is a big difference between building a mound and throwing up a heap of dirt. (Cheers.) I say this to you about Afflatus; he will be building them upside-down next. (Loud laughter.) And what about the roads! What about the mounds if there is no road to get to them! When I charged him with this, what said then the Honourable Afflatus? He said, "We build for posterity; let posterity worry about the roads." I have said to Afflatus, "Posterity is just around the corner." But did Afflatus build roads? Hell, no! Afflatus was too busy riding around. Afflatus was too busy hiring comely maidens to keep the records of what he calls his administration. How many of these maidens actually work for Afflatus? It might be worth your while to ask. (Prolonged applause.)

Vesuvius, Caesar, Eagle-Feather! Heroic figures these, which only Sarah could conceive. They tower as giants across the plains. But Sarah had too fine a sense of literary values to be always in the heroic mood. There are passages in *The Magma* of lilting beauty, as in *Now it is Done*. There are quiet pastoral scenes, as in *Omniscient Plan*. There are pictures of merry-making, as in *Square Dance*, of the husbandman at work, as in *Hiawatha's Milking*. There is that touching tribute to motherhood in *Little Papoose*. There is above all that stupendous blast of prairie wind, *Storm at Sea*. As yet these are but fragments of the larger picture which must still be pierced together. But what fragments!

Of those cantos of *Up from the Magma* which have already been read the best known is that dealing with the Red Brother of the plains, *Canto IV, The Skin Age*. Sarah, still shovelling, had by this time, and with the aid of Warden and Rockbuster, from whose text whole passages had been lifted bodily and set to verse, exposed the whole geological structure of Saskatchewan. But geology, as we know, was to her only the background of the future. Already she had written,

> In schist, and schistose rocks are writ the bans,
> For him whose eye can Runic read, and cast
> The other optic upward till it spans,
> In tortured gaze the future and the past:
> For such a one that panoramic view
> Shows rock to soil, and soil to groat and greens—
> Nay, such a one already smells the stew
> Of beet and barley bubbling with the beans.

The inner eye, the inner nose—it matters little with which faculty the poet is most endowed. To divine the future or to recreate the past was, for Sarah, all in a day's work. But in the case of *The Skin Age* she had at least one foot in the present. Here she was on something very close to the home grounds.

Sixteen miles north of Willows lay the thriving town of Quagmire. Immediately north of Quagmire's own Railroad Avenue, and extending for half a mile into the open prairie, lay the hundred or more scattered cabins of the Macdonalds and the Robideauxs, all that was left in Sarah's experience of the Red Brother of the plains. But it was enough. Ole had been there, and—in his younger days—her grandfather had been there quite often. Even Sarah, on the day of the Quagmire Agricultural Society Fair, had made it a point—since she had arrived in Quagmire that day even before the Midway Special train—to wander north of Railroad Avenue into what the Quagmire citizens tolerantly referred to as "the reservation." With such first-hand, or almost first-hand, experience of the Red Brother, some of them, to quote Jacob Binks, "pretty dam' pale," Sarah had little difficulty in visualizing the Ojibway-Cree at his romantic best.

It is on the basis of Sarah's first-hand experience of the Red Brother that we may dismiss at once the suggestion of P. S. Urchin-Smith [1] that Sarah would likely have written *Canto IV, The Skin Age* in the original Ojibway as she had written *Canto III* in Mound-Builder, were it not for the fact that the language of the Ojibway-Cree had, with far-sighted intention, been so constructed that no two words would rhyme. Sarah would have rhymed it anyway. Her knowledge of the Mound Builders is admittedly somewhat vague, but she employs the best medium in which to express herself, even as in her Darkest Africa her poetry becomes uncertain and confused—but still English. And where she has solid material to work on as in the case of the Red Brother, it is very definitely English. She could not have written *Canto IV* in any other language than that in which her thoughts and experiences were framed.

The Skin Age opens appropriately enough with a lyric to an Ojibway maiden—"a tone picture of infinite felicity", according to Miss Rosalind Drool, "done in miniature."

> Patrick O'Neil O'Connell,
> Late of the Mounted Police,
> And Moon-in-the-Eyes Macdonald,
> Are blessed, but not by the priest;
>
> For Patrick O'Neil in a glib way
> Has spoken to Moon-in-the-Eyes,
> And her answers in English-Ojibway,
> Were not what the padre advised;
>
> For although Moon might choose a cathedral,
> A blessing, a book, and a prayer—
> She's going to be dodecahedral,
> Since Patrick's a bit off the square.

It is a charming little thing, and Miss Rosalind Drool has made much of it. Even Dr Taj Mahal has been attracted by its

---

[1] Urchin-Smith, *Adventures in Philology, Ashcan*, Vol. 6, No. 6.

geometrical possibilities and declares that it needs figuring out.

In writing *The Skin Age*, in fact in writing *The Magma* generally, Sarah must undoubtedly have received considerable inspiration from Grandfather Thurnow. It was one thing to have visited Quagmire or to have observed the Red Brother on his occasional visits to Willows, but for their lore and romantic tradition she drew more often than not upon the unplumbed depths of the old man's memory. His was a bottomless reservoir of experience enriched with meditation and philosophical reflection—and turnipin. Only the poetic quality, the tender, the heroic, the lyrical, was lacking, and these Sarah, and only Sarah could supply. With *Eagle-Feather*, "that gaunt shadow of valour summoned from Saskatchewan's glorious past," she must have derived much of its material from her grandfather's—or perhaps even Ole's—frequent trips to Quagmire. But in *Little Papoose* Sarah is definitely on her own. No account of either grandfather's or Ole's visits to the reservation could have suggested—quite the contrary, in fact—that sweet picture of motherhood. It is one of infinite charm. It shows the Algonquin mother singing her infant daughter—undoubtedly a daughter—to sleep as the creeping twilight "draws its shadows across the skies." She sings, and as she sings, she gives the child a little nourishment from time to time to induce its slumber.

> Little Papoose, the twilight creeping,
> Draws its shadows across the skies—
> Another hour and you'll be sleeping—
> Here's a pickle, close your eyes.

> Little Papoose, the daylight passes,
> And soon the night will be full of dreams—
> And you'll be full of bread and molasses,
> And stewed dried apples and tinned sardines.

> Little Papoose, the night grows blacker,
> And you'll be round as a young balloon,
> With two cups of tea, and fifteen crackers,
> And a double handful of saskatoons.

On the reservation or off it, Sarah never permits the Red Brother to wander far from the farm. When he goes astray, as in *West Wind*, where Squawking-Hawk goes to town with his treaty money for "a bottle of lemon and three of vanilla", she quickly brings him home;

> "Blow him, West Wind, that his going,
> May be coming back to me,
> Speed him, West, or he'll be blowing
> All he's paid for being Cree."

calls the Ojibway maiden to her lover, and he returns "swift as an arrow but not as straight." The same is true of *Hunter's Moon*, where the Ojibway maiden calls her lover from his hunting,

> Red Brother, Red Brother,
> Wandering wild and free—
> Tonight it's hunter's moon, Brother—
> How about hunting me!

> Hunter's moon is low, Brother,
> Hang up the bow of wood—
> And hunter's moon will show, Brother
> Where the hunting's good.

> Hunter's moon is pale, Brother,
> And hark—from bush and nook,
> A wild voice calls, Brother,
> You won't have long to look.

Not all the verses are being quoted here. Miss Rosalind Drool, who is officially credited with its discovery in *The Magma*, has permitted her sweeping admiration of this poem to carry her beyond the reading of it into the actual addition of several verses of her own, and this fact has made it difficult, according to Professor Marrowfat, "to decide which is Binks and which is Drool."

In *Hiawatha's Milking*, the Red Brother, no longer wandering, is back at his chores. Sarah, who generally contents herself with the more simple quatrains, here breaks into a new verse pattern, more, it is said, to puzzle her critics as to

its source than for any need of new literary form. This is un-
likely. Sarah was only too well aware that the milking of a
Saskatchewan cow calls always for new forms of expression.
On this occasion she uses trochaics:

HIAWATHA'S MILKING

Give me of your milk, oh moo-cow,
Of your pure white juice, oh do, cow,
Reasonably white and not too blue, cow
Give me rich white milk, oh Flossie,
She whom men sometimes call Bossy,
She whom men sometimes call Co-boss,
Sometimes So-boss, sometimes Whoa-boss,
Kick not me, nor pail, I pray, cow,
Or I'll bust you one from here to Cracow:
And the cow, whom men call Co-boss,
Sometimes So-boss, sometimes Whoa-boss,
Shuddering in all its branches,
Trembling like the wild Comanches,
Turned upon him eyes of doleful,
Eyes of sadness, eyes of soulful,
Breathing deeply to inhale full,
Kicked him neatly in the pail-full,
Slapped him 'cross the face with tail-full,
Saying with a sigh of sorrow,
"Take the milk, oh Hi, tomorrow,
Take my milk, oh Hiawatha,
Try and get it Hiawatha!"

There is action here, but it is subdued. Co-boss alone
appears to hold the stage and Hiawatha plays a more or less
passive role. His is more in the nature of an invocation, a
hope expressed—and crushed. Sarah sensed this and shared
in his defeat. Even Co-boss seems to sense it; "Eyes of doleful,
eyes of soulful," is not mere rhetoric. An age was passing. A
culture was going down. Slowly the page of history was being
turned upon the Red Brother and all he stood for. The long
paths—"the uncharted paths"—were the way of his feet, and
although he might yet stand for a passing day, even as stood
Eagle Feather, in the end Sarah must needs salute that heroic
figure with a tear.

EAGLE FEATHER

Salute with a tear the great departed,
Give solemn thoughts and a sigh for them—
And for Eagle Feather, on paths uncharted,
Sing appropriate requiem :
Sing the nook where he had his hour,
Sing the Eagle, his best and worst—
Here's where he stood like the leaning tower,
Lost in his thoughts—and his cosmic thirst;
  Sing that impassive face of leather—
Silent, inscrutable, Eagle Feather!

Gone from his quoin 'til his days are counted,
Carried away to a new frontier—
He mixed it up with the North-West Mounted—
Eagle Feather has got a year—
A year and a day—but a day worth telling—
With the surge of battle deep within—
Mothers screaming—fathers yelling—
(Somebody gave him a quart of gin)
  Sing that day—and his year—together—
Back on the war-path—Eagle Feather!

Back to the war-whoop, shrill and throaty,
Back to the buffalo—back to the plains—
Chase, and be chased by the wild coyote—
Plug the pale-face—scalp the remains—
Back to the bow—and the covered wagon—
Back—The Eagle—Chief for the day—
And back to the joy of the white man's flagon—
Eagle Feather has been put away :
  Here's where he stood, in wind and weather—
Gone from his haunts is Eagle Feather.

Eagle Feather is true to the finest traditions of the West.
Sarah, keenly aware of this, gave it everything she had—
suspense, dramatic intensity, action—above all action,
quickened and sustained by "Somebody gave him a quart of
gin." For one brief moment the page of history is again
lifted, and across it stalks Eagle Feather, splendid, confident,
arrogant, a symbol again of Saskatchewan's most glorious
past. Nor has Saskatchewan failed to recognize its greatness.

Year after year, with unfailing regularity it has been placed on the List of Supplementary Reading for the Schools.

With the closing of *Canto IV, The Skin Age*, Sarah took a day off. She was feeling faintly unwell.

Concerning the other nine cantos of *Up from the Magma*, together with the Prologue, the Epilogue, the Index, and the full-page illustration of the thirteen Schwantzhacker sisters, little can be said. Certainly, with the exception of Canto XIII, no coherent literary account can as yet be given. They have not all been read. The scholars of literature cannot be called strictly to account. After all, to read a full cubic foot of closely written manuscript and to translate one complete canto from Mound-Builder into English, is no light task. Sarah's manuscript also presents an additional difficulty in that her thought or verse is frequently carried over to the other side of the page, where—except to the most earnest and dedicated scholar—it tends to become lost among the domestic confusion of the articles which are being put up for auction. Moreover, there are some splendid bargains in Tax Sales and under Chattel Mortgage Foreclosures, and these, emphasized by the unvarying succession of four or five hundred pages before changing to several hundred pages of an even better bargain, must be regarded as no inconsiderable factor in the literary scholars also taking a day off.

Under such handicaps there must always be a certain amount of surmise and speculation. And just what Sarah Binks had in mind when she entitled the next canto, *The Roman Occupation*, we do not fully know. Scholars are agreed that it may be necessary to read the entire canto before we do. The suggestion has been made that Sarah's attendance at the Willows school was frequently interrupted by the extra chores following Ole's own attendance at political meetings of national importance, and that Sarah may easily have been at school on those days in which British history was being taught while under the impression that it was still Canadian. It is a common error, and the suggestion may not readily be dismissed. But even though we grant the possibility of Sarah having mixed her two histories, it seems odd that she should have placed the Roman Occupation after the Ojibway-Cree in point of time. A somewhat plausible explanation offered by Taj Mahal is that Sarah got not her histories but the numbering of her pages mixed. This would be unusual for Sarah. She may have been weak in history, but as the daughter of Jacob Binks she could certainly count.

Sarah, after all, was writing not a history but a literature. And regardless of where she put, or perhaps intended to put, the Roman Occupation, in a way it meant digging Saskatchewan out all over again. Having regard for her own recollection in the back yard, an age of pottery shards, which for her meant "broken flower pots and cups without handles mixed with ashes," and bronze coins "with which you can't buy anything in this country," was hardly what her sense of the dramatic unities called for. Sarah was not going to do all that shovelling for nothing. She therefore slurs over this aspect of the Roman Occupation, and it is quite possible that had her grandfather been able to help her with the language as he had done with Mound-Builder, she would have written this canto in Roman.

What had captured Sarah's imagination was the Romans themselves. She saw them always in terms of dignity and greatness. It had been no indifferent compliment to the Premier to have cast him in the role of Cincinnatus, or to have given the Hired Man "knees, like Hercules' ". And the entrance of Caesar into Saskatchewan, together with the admiring chorus of the bystanders as to his rank and privilege, is attended with all the pomp and splendour of the Honourable Grafton Tabernackel opening the Quagmire Agricultural Society Fair:

> Here comes Caesar! Pound the drums!
> Blow the bagpipes! Caesar comes!
> Crowd the platform! Pull up tight!
> That's him—the Honourable Caesar, alright,
> The one with the badge, and the bag of fixtures,
> Yep, that's Caesar—just like his pictures!
> His are the cares, and the joys of state—
> A good man to know—and to emulate.

> (*Chorus of the Bystanders;*)
> Caesar is Caesar, for all that's in it,
> A job on the census, a seat in the senate.
> An office East, a farm on the prairie,
> A pass on the train with his secretary,
> A yacht on the bay, a band like Sousa's
> And a suite full of starry-eyed lallapaloozas.

What Sarah meant by the "bag of fixtures" we again do not know. That it "began to leak", we are told in the second verse just after the line

"Some kid gives him a bunch of pansies,"

but no one can be sure. Sarah has a disconcerting habit of using a term in some unusual or special sense in her treatment of the Romans, and sometimes she herself is not sure of their meaning, and admits it. "What ho, lictor, whatever that is," she declares frankly in *Lictor, Clear The Way*. Evidently by the time this fragment was written the Roman occupation was going ahead as well as could be expected.

LICTOR, CLEAR THE WAY

What ho, lictor, whatever that is,
Clear the way with mattock, saw,
Slash the scrub where the lurking rat is,
Catamount, cut-worm, courriere de bois,
Lay out streets, perspiring hewer,
Level them off with scoop and claw,
Point the way for a road and sewer,
A legislature, and Roman law.

No one seems to find out exactly what lictor [1] or lictor's

---

[1] An interesting comment which throws some light on the possible meaning of the word *lictor*, comes from one of the retired old-timers of Quagmire, Josiah Sweetings, who for years was associated with the development of Regina. When *Lictor, Clear the Way*, was first read to him by press representatives, he is reported to have said:

"Roman law is right! It must have been back in 1911 or 1912. A group of us had formed a small syndicate to take up where the Romans left off. Cut-worms didn't bother us none, and this development wasn't out far enough to run into courriere de bois. But catamounts! Boy! There was one in particular whom the men used to call Rosie. And was she a hell-cat, or was she a hell-cat! This was supposed to be high-class residential stuff, and we had to buy her out—goodwill and all. Looking back I'd say that Rosie was the only one who ever made any money out of that development. I sometimes wonder who was *lictor* and who was licked in that whole game. Certainly not one of us has a damn cent now."

job is in this development, but he is a hard worker and Sarah keeps him at it. Saskatchewan must have been booming again at that time.

It may be that Sarah's spelling is sometimes at fault. Just as she had previously used the word, balsam, where she probably meant balm, so in *Balbus Will Pluck A Grape*, she uses the Roman word for corn, *frumentum*, where the context clearly calls for the English, fermentum. The context here appears to be a Roman festival or picnic celebrating the first ripening of the native fruits of Saskatchewan. Sarah probably got the recipe for the frumentum from her grandfather.

BALBUS WILL PLUCK A GRAPE

Balbus will pluck a grape! My friends,
This ceremony marks the season's turning:
We gather here to greet the day that ends
A long protracted drought and inner yearning—
For lo, the year has rolled, and once again
Balbus selects the first symbolic berry—
In this great cornucopia of plain,
Nature at least is lavish in choke-cherry.

Once more will flow the sweet, new, prairie wine,
In over-proof of eighty-five percentum—
Potato, saskatoon, and dandelion,
And turnip have been blended in frumentum—
And these—with cherry—give a mixture which
Is guaranteed to kill at forty rods—
Or free, in all-time high of sound and pitch,
A song in praise of bacchus and the gods.[1]

With "A legislature and Roman law" Saskatchewan had finally come into its own. Sarah, no doubt, pays it fitting tribute. She must have, or she could not have written all

---

[1] A rather curious note in connection with this poem comes from Urchin-Smith, (*Adventures in Philology*, Loc. Cit.) He points out that in spelling Bacchus with a small *b*, Sarah may have had in mind not a person but a place. Intriguing!

those other cantos. But *Up from the Magma* is still the un-opened treasure house of Saskatchewan's literature. Sooner or later it will be read completely and there is no doubt that some of Sarah's finest work still lies buried among the Tax Sales and Mortgage Foreclosures. Even paging quickly through them, say a hundred or two hundred pages at a time, the reader's attention is arrested by lines of lilting beauty or vivid action. Taking it more slowly, say fifty or even twenty-five pages at a time, one comes across quiet pastoral scenes or poems of deep reflective power and insight. Only a few can be quoted here. The unopened treasure house—Marrowfat calls it "untapped"—must wait its real day. As yet the tendency is to go through it five hundred to a thousand pages at a time.

Such eagerness does a dis-service to Sarah. Literature must be savoured, not gulped. Sarah herself took a whole winter to write *The Magma*, and for once in her experience it was a winter of content. True, she had shovelled—and it had been hard. But in the end she had uncovered that hidden good—and more. For literature it was Saskatchewan; for herself—above all for herself—it was mastery, it was judgement, it was achievement. She sums it all up, both for Saskatchewan and for herself in those amazing lines—those shining lines—

The man whose tile has almost reached its ending.
Whose coat is gone, and vest beyond repair,
Whose stately pantaloons are long past mending,
And shirt and undershirt admit the air;
The man whose shoes have lost their first new splendour,
And gaping, mock the passer-by with toe—
Such man has difficulty to engender
The confidence of those who run the show :
But let him to his home—and on the morrow
Adorn himself in lavender and spat,
And cover up his pantaloons, and borrow
From neighbours a Prince Albert and a hat—
Then show himself, and if so be his nature
To stand and talk within the public marts—
They gladly send him to the legislature,
Or mark him judge and critic of the arts.

And who can help but feel for Sarah—and for Saskatchewan!

Not all *The Magma* is of such reflective power and deep insight. *Square Dance*, (about a hundred pages at a time) is as light and fanciful—"full of lilt and tilt," according to Miss Drool—as anything Sarah had ever written. It is almost as if she were harking back to the *Grizzlykick Symphony*, but nothing there, not even *Hi Sooky*, approaches it in swing and swish. It is said that Sarah had Mathilda and Ole go through the steps on the kitchen floor while her grandfather played the mouth-organ and "called", while she herself dashed off the poem, keeping time with her foot. If so, it could only have been to recall a larger setting. The poem is too crowded with character for such a small kitchen. We know for certain that there was a dance in Willows that winter, and Sarah probably attended in her usual capacity as observer. She was never one to enter actively into the social life—no poet is. If she had been, there might have been enough partners to go around and the obliging Malarty, "with a handkerchief tied to his wing," would have slipped back to the livery stable and surrendered his place in literature to Sarah who certainly had no use for it by this time.

SQUARE DANCE [1]

Sing ho, for the dance,
To shuffle and prance,
Sing "Ladies, do-si-do!"
And fiddles engage,
With "Bird-in-the-cage",
Sing, "Eleben-left!"—Sing ho!
Give me the square,
When harmonicas blare,
And the ladies are set for the swing—
And Squiffy Malarty
Has made up the party,
With a handkerchief tied to his wing:

---

[1] The discovery of *Square Dance* has been credited to James Cordite Bantam; (*Folk Lore and Folk Dances of the Submarginal Areas of Western Canada*, Bulletin 46, Adult Education Series, Manitoba, 1940)

Swing Olga, swing Lena,
Swing Kate and Katrina,
Swing Gudrun, and Bjorg, and Gertrude,
Swing heavy, swing hearty,
Swing Squiffy Malarty,
The life of the party—and stewed.

Give me the dance,
Where the girls take a chance,
With seam and with button and string,
And swing them up higher,
Before they retire—
Sing ho, heigh-ho, for the swing;
Sing ho, for the swirls,
And the breathless girls,
With the swimming delight in their eyes—
Come smaller or taller,
Take off the collar—
Sing ho, for the exercise;

Swing Daisy, swing Betty,
Swing Maisie and Letty,
Swing Mirabel, Margie, and Joy,
Swing Mrs McGinty,
Six feet and squinty,
Two hundred and twenty—and coy.

Sarah was not unsocial. But the poet cannot both observe
the stream of life and swim in it. This is at once his tragedy
and his reward. He is conscious of an inner integrity, but
aware too that this integrity must, in its very nature, be an
integrity of isolation. Having its roots in the social body, the
poetic spirit must nevertheless stand apart from it, longing
to enter but unable to do so.[1] And the poet thus torn but

---

[1] This point is repeatedly emphasized in the writings of the
"Regina School" of poets, as witness Wraitha Dovecote's, *The
Poet's Prayer*. (Republished by permission of the Editors of *Plush*.)

Oh Lord, who holdest in thy hand
The gift of triolet and ode,
Or sonnet none can understand,
And rhymeless lines of current mode,
Whose reservoir of thought still brims

seeking always a universality, turns as often as not to nature for his solace. What he finds there depends upon the intensity of an inner conflict whose issues may not even be explicitly stated in awareness. And Sarah, "Sarah, the Woman," but every inch the poetess, may have had such an attack following *Square Dance*. Only thus can we explain, *Storm at Sea*, in which for one brief moment in her whole literary career she sees nature in its harshest aspect—hostile, savage, cruel.

STORM AT SEA

A hail, for the sailor who puts to sea,
When the wind is right, and the sky is free;
But shed a tear for his sweetheart true,
If he isn't home in a month or two—
But shed more tears for the sailor lad,
When the wind is east—and the weather's bad;
    Then it's into your woolies
    And heave, my bullies,
    And wind up the sails,
    And pull on the pullies,
    And shout together, Ship Ahoy—
    It's going to blow—and boy, oh boy!
The storm clouds gather, the rigging hums,
The captain shudders—and here she comes—
Ripping the shingles from off the deck,
The wind grows louder and louder, by Heck—
Ah, many a vessel has been submersed,
And gone to the bottom, caboose-end first—

    With bright ideas when mine are spent—
    Guard Thou the rondels and the hymns,
    Of me, Thy humble instrument;
      Defend from attitude and mime,
    The metered thought, and lead the wit,
    From obvious and facile rhyme,
    And unexpected ending's pit—
    Above all, may I never take,
    Albeit light, the cynic's view
    That love is always on the make—
    However true, however true.

So it's heave, my hearties,
And yell, my hearties,
And slug and batter the bell, my hearties,
And send out the S. O. L. my hearties,
The storm is at its worst.

Ah, many a sailor, when help is past,
Has gone to the bottom, caboose-end last,
And many a weeping sweetheart true,
Has counted and waited a month or two,
Has counted and waited a month at least,
And written him off as predeceased—
So belay, my buddy,
And stay, my buddy,
And let them bloody-well weigh, my buddy,
And stay or stow away, my buddy,
When the wind is turning east.

There we have it—tragedy. Tragedy, and the long wait—
"a month at least." It is the age-long story of man against
the elements.

Why did Sarah Binks write *Storm at Sea*? The sea, after
all, is Ole's sea, or grandfather's sea, or anybody's sea, and
the brave sailors are true to the nautical tradition in not
sending out the S. O. L. until it is too late. But the wind—
the wind is a prairie wind, a Saskatchewan wind. And Sarah,
ever since the day of the Quagmire Agricultural Society Fair
had promised herself never to write another word about the
wind as long as she lived. It had been a surrender, a defeat—
and Sarah knew it. Always that wind had defeated her and
it always would. And she knew, too, that long after she herself was gone, long after Saskatchewan itself had been blown
back into the geological dust from which she had unshovelled
it in so many arduous cantos, that that wind would still
blow—persistent, unyielding, powerful. But one last gesture
she must make. One last fling of defiance in the face of that
eternal challenge. Man against the gods! Sarah against the
Saskatchewan wind! She might go down under it, but she
would go down asserting herself as something finally and
ultimately greater—the poetic spirit flaunting itself before
the destinies. What premonitions she may have had at this
hour we can never know. But this we know, that in writing

Storm at Sea at this stage of her career, she was true, not alone to herself, but to the finest traditions of poetry in every age and clime.

The effort must have wearied her, *Storm at Sea* is the last poem of any consequence in *The Magma*. Hesitatingly, almost falteringly, she closes her great work with four lines from an old Mission Song—not even her own;

> "Now is the last spike driven,
> Now is the last tie riven,
> Now is the last speech given—
> Let's all go home!"

II

Sarah, The Woman

Up from *The Magma and Back Again* won the Wheat Pool Medal. Say what we will of Sarah's genius, acclaim her as the Sweet Songstress of Saskatchewan, the Poet's Poetess, or simply as Sarah, the Woman, this spontaneous and unsolicited bestowal of the highest honour in the land will always place her in the van of that never-ending stream of poets which next to cereals is Saskatchewan's greatest contribution to the big, open spaces. Never again was the Wheat Pool Medal to be bestowed for poetry. "Once is enough," declared the Hon. A. E. Windheaver in pinning the medal to Sarah's breast and tying his handkerchief around his thumb; "Once, and once only has this honour been bestowed for poetry. This great organization, the Wheat Pool, together with my good friends of Willows and district and the electors as far south as Pelvis and as far north as Quagmire who have asked me to act as their representative on this occasion because they were not sure that they could get here over the roads which have been promised for the last four years although thousands of dollars of the taxpayer's money has been spent, join me today in bestowing this honour upon you, Miss Binks, or shall I call you Sarah Binks, because I want my friends to know me as I know them, join me today and we are proud of you and Saskatchewan is proud of you and if there were more like you and if the Ladies of this district would get together and organize for a good, clean government, I think I could get another honour for this district, and if the new Post Office which I spoke of before is ever built I think I could get some of your verses emblazoned on it in letters of imperishable bronze or carved in gleaming tablets of immortal stone, or at least concrete, if we ever get a government that has the interests of the people at heart and not just riding around on free passes and blowing the taxpayer's money."

Letters of imperishable bronze! Tablets of immortal stone! Alas, the horse thermometer! Already in this moment of Sarah's greatest triumph Death had marked that shining mark for its own soon aim and the daisies were burgeoning restlessly, nay, impatiently in the sod. The ringing words of the Honourable A. E. Windheaver, himself long since called to his reward in the Canadian Senate, were not to find their splendid realization when the new Post Office was finally built. But Sarah Binks had written her name upon the soil of Saskatchewan, she had carved her words into the hearts of the people.

The award of the Wheat Pool Medal was no mere honour to be won in competition with others, no subscriptions to be sold or portraits of Adolf McCohen to collect. It was even more than the acclaim of Sarah's genius as a poetess. That had been established. It was a tribute, a spontaneous recognition of Sarah Binks as a public character, as a woman, and as a producer. Above all as a producer. Production was the motto and slogan of the Pool, production and a controlled market. And when the directors of the Wheat Pool made the announcement that their annual medal that year would be given in the Willows-Quagmire district to the one who had shown the greatest productive activity and asked for nominations, what name but that of Sarah Binks, the authoress of a cubic foot of *Up from the Magma and Back Again* would come first to mind. It had been a drought year and production in almost every other respect had reached new lows. True, at the Clarendon Hotel it had been suggested that Kurt Schwantzhacker, a father and a taxpayer, would be considered, but it would appear—Mathilda, his youngest, was now eighteen—that his producing days were over. Moreover, the medal carried with it no cash award. Honour begets honour; Sarah had won the McCohen and Meyers competition, then why not the Wheat Pool Medal. If the Willows-Quagmire district were to qualify at all, then why not Sarah Binks, the Poetess, the Woman. Her market was very definitely a controlled one, her productive activity amazing.

Indeed, posterity may well ask, why not Sarah Binks. There was never any real doubt as to her qualifications.

Sarah was henceforth to belong to Saskatchewan for all times. The Reeve and Councillors of the Municipality of North Willows, and the Associated Boards of Trade of Quagmire and Pelvis, were unanimous in nominating Sarah Binks, the author of *Up from the Magma and Back Again* to the honour of the Wheat Pool Medal and moved that nominations close. Nor did the directors of the Wheat Pool hesitate. The Secretary was asked to read *Up from the Magma and Back Again* and to bring in a favourable report. Indeed, the minutes of the annual meeting of the Wheat Pool indicate that the entire poem, on the motion of the chairman, "be taken as read", and is so recorded.

Sarah wrote two poems for the occasion of the presentation of the medal. One is a personal tribute to the Hon. A. E. Windheaver, who made the presentation, and the other a gracious and graceful tribute to the Saskatchewan farmer, which, with a fine sense of fitness she dedicates to her father. It is one of her deeply reflective works in which she shows the attachment of the farmer for and to the soil, and discusses the finely adjusted balance of nature;

TO MY FATHER, JACOB BINKS

I used to think the cut-worm and the weevil,
Were things that blindly come and go by chance,
And Hessian-fly an undiluted evil,
To make the farmer shudder in his pants;
But now I know they hold him to his acre,
For could he ever win and take his ease,
He'd up and leave his binder and his breaker,
And give the precious land back to the Crees.

I used to think the beetle and the hopper
Were but a pest, but now I realize
That French-weed as a yield is right and proper,
And cut-worms are a blessing in disguise;
That rust, and hail, and stem-rot are protection,
And what we call the drought year is a means
To keep the farmer on his quarter section,
Although it makes him tremble in his jeans.

The things that we call trials are a warning,
The thing we call the gopher is a boon,
For should a crop appear some early morning,
The farmer would be gone by afternoon;
The hopper should be cherished and be shielded,
And Hessian fly is something we should trust—
If what we call the crop is ever yielded,
You'll never see the farmer for his dust.

It is a poem which definitely places her among the Immortals.

The actual presentation of the Wheat Pool Medal has been described by the special correspondents of *The Hitching Post* and the Quagmire *Influential*, both under the heading, NEW POST OFFICE FOR WILLOWS. Sarah, we are told, wore her white dress for the occasion, and Ole and Jacob Binks occupied positions of prominence on the stage together with a group of representative citizens and the Committee in charge of the arrangements. The *Influential* gives the Hon. A. E. Windheaver's speech in full and also reprints Sarah's tribute to that statesman which she recited after receiving the medal:

TO THE HONOURABLE A. E. WINDHEAVER

I left this place an ignorant youth,
In homespun shirt and fortunes wrecked,
But came back wiser than my fondest hope
Could have led me to expect;
My voice is heard where conglomerate men,
My name in the Government books,
And I have fine frock-coat, striped pants, and a vest,
And keen, intellectual looks.

The account in *The Hitching Post* (which at that time was Conservative, but has since become in quick succession United Farmer, C.C.F., Reconstruction, Social Credit, Birth Control, Vegetarian, and Liberal) omits to mention the presence of the Honourable Windheaver, but reprints in full the dedication to Jacob Binks, and is unstinting in its praise of the Wheat Pool.

Of particular interest and significance is the editorial in *The* (Willows) *Sheet*, under the heading, LOCAL GIRL MAKES GOOD.

The high place in the world of letters which our own Sarah Binks, daughter of Jacob Binks, the Chairman of the School Board, has carved for herself, culminating in the highest honour which it is the privilege of Sask atchewan to bestow, will always be a source of satis faction and pride to the people of this community. The large crowds which gathered last Wednesday to attend the ceremony at which she received the Wheat Pool Medal from one of this Province's most distinguished hands, attest to the interest in poetry and to the ad miration which her published work has received. But to us, the citizens of Willows and surrounding district this presentation is more than the mere acknowledge ment of her ability as a poetess. There are many of us who have never, and probably never will read her greatest work, *Up from the Magma and Back Again* said to be very powerful. The crowds, therefore, that gathered last Wednesday afternoon in the skating rink as well as those which gathered in the two overflow meetings at the Clarendon Hotel and the Commercial House, at which Sarah's kinsman, Thadeus T. Thurnow, consented to preside, speak all the more eloquently of the personal esteem in which our local poetess is held by all. To us, Sarah Binks is more than the winner of the Wheat Pool Medal. To us, she is one of ourselves She has grown up among us, attended our school, and done most of her shopping at our stores. We have seen her grow from the first grade into young womanhood Some of us have read her poems and followed her literary career, and all of us have followed her trip to Regina with more than usual interest. In so far as she was able to take time off from poetry she has taken her part in community affairs, and the geological trend which is said to mark her powerful epic is a direct result of her desire to serve this district with oil. The picturesque farm of our esteemed fellow citizen, Jacob Binks, owes much to the care and assistance of his talented daughter, and if there is anyone in this district of her age and weight who can spread or pitch better than she can the Editor would be glad to hear of it and to give due credit in these columns. Her interest in farm animals won for her the McCohen and Meyers competition and she has always been more than generous in loaning her thermometer. More than one family in this district has been saved the expense of a doctor when they thought they were sick owing to her thoughtfulness and her experience in taking temperatures.

Her words to the former Minister of Foreign Affairs and Grasshopper Control were well chosen. But her words, *To My Father, Jacob Binks*, are not merely tribute to any man. They are addressed to all of us, from one of us. We are proud to honour Sarah Binks, the winner of the Wheat Pool Medal. But it is Sarah, as a woman, as a member of the community, who has always interested us most and has won a place in our hearts. It is all the more regrettable, therefore, that on an occasion like this, the town of Willows should not be able to hold its meetings in a regular hall instead of in a skating rink where the sun beating down on the tin roof makes for poor ventilation and the school children rolling rocks on the tin roof makes for poor acoustics.

Sarah, the Poetess! Sarah, the Woman! Of all the lavish praise which poured upon her after the Wheat Pool Medal, this simple tribute from the home town paper, *The Sheet*, was the only one apparently, which she really valued and the only clipping she preserved. Although quite aware of her position in the world of letters, and of herself as a public character, she was too much her own severe critic to be moved by fulsome praise. But to be counted as a member of the Willows community moved her deeply. Her interest in community affairs had been more abstract than real, certainly, her probings with William Greenglow into the geology of the Binks' farm had been actuated more by an academic curiosity to discover what lay under the surface than by a desire to supply the community with oil. Sarah had what the philosophers call "the inquiring mind", but she also had considerable artistic aloofness, and had played more or less a lone hand as all poets must. As the only daughter of the somewhat taciturn Jacob Binks who permitted her to have her way in all things, and surrounded on all sides by masculine influences if we except Mathilda, whom she dominated, she had grown up independent, even headstrong, and had followed her own lines of development without which her latent genius could never have blossomed. And now she was made suddenly aware of a community around her, a community which claimed her as its own. To be regarded as Sarah Binks, W.P.M., the eminent poetess, she could understand and accept as her right, to be singled out as Sarah, the Woman whose progress into womanhood had been watched from the first grade, and whose trip to Regina had been followed "with more than usual interest", was to her a revelation and a challenge, and to some extent a reproach. She felt that she had neglected the community, whereas the community had kept a sharp eye on her.

The appeal to Sarah's community spirit found its immediate response in a poem which showed that she could take an even greater interest in community affairs than she had been given credit for. She wrote *Wash Out on the Line*,[1] published very appropriately in the home town paper, *The Sheet*. It is a poem in which Sarah, the Woman, earns her title. If she had had any misgivings as to her position in the community she was henceforth to have none; "If this doesn't fix me in this community," she writes to Mathilda in sending over a copy of the manuscript, "nothing will."

WASH OUT ON THE LINE

The sun is bright, and once again it's Monday,
And on each line the apron and the undie,
And tablecloth and towel adorning fence,
Tell family history and the week's events
In simple code, that he who runs, may read,
For passing fancy or his neighbour's need;
And changing calendar of underthing,
Remarks the winter or announces spring:

---

[1] WASH OUT ON THE LINE has since been set to music and adopted as the official marching song of the United Brotherhood of Railway Firemen.

Already in McGinty's yard the brevies
Nod in the wind to Joe McGinty's heavies;
And at the Brown's the extra sheet and best,
Flutters its tale of late departing guest;
And at the Jones'—another wash on Friday—
Announcement made in diaper and didy,
They now have six—at Smith's Salina's back—
Judged from her things, she must have got the sack.

Each line unfolds its bit of news or lack;
Here the new school ma'am spends it on her back,
Her lavender flimsies in the breezes beckon;
She won't last long in this town, I reckon;
And Mrs Pete Cattalo is getting stout;
Pete had an extra shirt this week, he's stepping out,
Must be the new Gimp girl, at her grandma's
A bit fast, too, Heavens, yes, pyjamas!

'Tis Monday morn, let each her message fling,
From stately tent-pole to the twisted string,
In terms of rinse, and bleach, and starch, and blueing,
Of fortune, charcter, or just what's doing.

It was Sarah's last poem [1]

It is useless to speculate as to what heights Sarah Binks might have reached had not Death touched her with his untimely finger. Dr Taj Mahal has derived a formula and drawn a curve based upon her productive activity during her last three years, which would seem to indicate that her work followed the law of squares, and that had she continued for another three years her annual literary output would have exceeded the total of any other writer, past or present. Miss Rosalind Drool, on the other hand, without regard to Sarah's literary potentialities, bewails her passing as, "a life which had not reached its complete fulfilment and fruition." Even Marrowfat is somewhat in accordance with this view. Though he appears to take some satisfaction in the thought that Sarah dead could produce no more poems, "hard enough to understand as they are," his regret is genuine when he states, "She showed all the signs of becoming a more interest-

---

[1] Incidentally, it was the last issue of The (Willows) Sheet.

ing woman." But the Author cannot altogether share these regrets, certainly not on the bases advanced. Mahal's method of extrapolation is a new approach to the literary problem and must be accepted with caution. It clearly indicates a great loss, but it must be pointed out that it takes into account only Sarah's potential yardage or cubic footage— Mahal, as usual, is uncertain of his units—and fails to take into account the question of *quality*, always an important consideration where poetry is involved. It may have been that Sarah, scaling the unclimbed peaks, could have reached an isolation of greatness where even Saskatchewan could not have understood her, and Professor Marrowfat, for once, seems to be stumbling towards the truth. But for Miss Drool to interpolate into what she calls, "The Unfinished Symphony of Sarah's life" another of the frustration complexes with which readers of all her work are only too familiar, is hardly in accordance with what we know of Sarah. There was nothing frustrated about Sarah. She had had her struggles and disappointments and her Darkest Africa. But she had won through to a horse thermometer and to the Wheat Pool Medal. She had studied geology, she had been to Regina. Who can say that she had not reached the fullness of life? Hers was the joy of sky and field and the driving rain against her cheek. She had health and vitality and the inner satisfaction of achievement. The community had claimed her—Saskatchewan called her its own.

In such a person the love of life is strong. But Sarah must have had some awareness of those very peaks of cold isolation to which her genius must ultimately have led her. The high resolve, Sarah's own, "To face these facts undismayed," which had carried her up the slopes and had plumbed the profound geological depths of N. E. ¼ Sec. 37, T. 21, R. 9, W. would never have permitted her to turn back. But one cannot but wonder whether Sarah's courage must not at times have faltered—she would not have been human otherwise. Certainly that disillusionment which is the concomitant of success would have been hers sooner or later. There is a suggestion of this in the one portrait we have of Sarah, taken a few months before her death. It shows her in thoughtful mood leaning far out of the window and gazing wonderingly, wistfully, over the prairies she loved so well. It may have been that she was casting her mind back to her childhood when she wandered those same prairies in search of flowers, or trudged, a little girl, her potato-bug and lunch pail under her arm, the mile and a quarter to the Willows school. This, at least, is the impression one gathers from a study of the portrait, an impression which might have been heightened if the photographer had taken the picture from outside instead of from within the room.

Alas, the horse thermometer! The gods of Greek drama must have laughed ironically when that fateful instrument, that first tangible mark of Sarah's success finally broke and proved to be the tragic means of her destruction. Mercury poisoning is a dreadful thing, but it is swift and sure, and as dramatically fitting as the asp and the hemlock. Sarah had reached the height of her powers and she was still far from the inevitable senility which besets all poets upon receiving recognition. But from her pinnacle she could look ahead and faintly she could hear the echo of that far cry from her Darkest Africa:

> This makes me scratch myself and ask,
> When shall my powers fade?
> It puts me severely to the task,
> To face this fact undismayed.

After all, what was the beauty of sky and field and rain-drenched hill, of prairie swept by storm, of dazzling alkali flat, of hot fallow land in the sun of the summer afternoon, of the misty pastels of spreading time? All these things had been hers, and yet not hers. They had entered into her and become part of her and she had caught some of their intangible spirit and flung it back: "Burbank, bobolink, and snearth" she had sung long ago in ecstasy of joy. But she knew that they could never be completely hers, that they belonged to the prairie and to the West, that they were of Saskatchewan for all time.

"This makes me scratch myself and ask"; the Fates weave their web of circumstance around the great. It is no mere coincidence that the great epidemic of hives which swept Saskatchewan should have found Sarah with a horse thermometer which registered six degrees too high. It is no mere coincidence that she had become passionately fond of Scotch mints, and bearing down upon one of them at a moment when she was taking her own temperature cracked the thermometer and swallowed the mercury, a full tablespoon, with a plop. There was no catching it. Death loves a shining mark; the Fates had tied the final knot in the web—and in Sarah. For her there was no escape.

The facts of Sarah Binks' death from mercury poisoning are too well known and tragic to bear a detailed repetition, and the Author, blinded by tears and things, prefers not to discuss it. Dr Taj Mahal, who has reconstructed her temperature chart from available data, and on the same chart has plotted the daily price of wheat during the epidemic,[1] claims that if the thermometer had ever been properly calibrated against a standard horse and corrections applied accordingly, then the root of Sarah's temperature plus pi minus eight would give the same values he found in her production curve. Genius will out!

One more honour still remained for Sarah. St Midget's conferred upon her the degree of Doctor of Laws, (*in absentia*). No provision had been made in the calendar of St Midget's for a posthumous degree, and so far no L.L.D. had been conferred upon anyone actually dead. But the always earnest desire of St Midget's to confer its honour upon those who had achieved success was able to surmount this fine distinction. Sarah would always live in the hearts of her countrymen.

Sarah Binks, W.P.M., L.L.D., The Sweet Songstress, the Poet's Poetess, the Woman! Who shall take her place? Some day, from the ever fertile soil of the West, another genius may spring. Some day, perhaps—some day! Until then—until then, let simple shaft of composition stone tell in that one word, forever eloquent, her place and her achievement—ALONE.

---

[1] The extent of this epidemic may be judged from the fact that at the Cactus Lake fair in the third heat of the 2.15 for two year olds and under, and in the second heat of the 3.45 for twelve year olds and over, all of the horses and several of the jockeys had to be scratched.

L'ENVOI

Oh I'll light my pipe no more
Where the dusty reapers roar,
   And the swishing, tossing waves of wheat
Stretch endless from the door;
Where the wind from off the fallow,
Warm and steady, soft and mellow,
   Brings the chorus of the crickets
From their moonlit dancing floor.

Oh I'll nevermore go back,
Where the granaries strain and crack,
   And at dusk, from fields returning
With their teams and empty racks,
Come the boys; the sound of pumping—
Running water—horses thumping
   In their stalls—and tired voices—
Hank and Ole, Bill and Mac'.

Oh the years have gone forever,
Hurdy gurdy, hubble-bubble,
But the autumn nights still bring me,
Like a breath across the stubble,
Like a land breeze in the tropics,
   Full of murmur and delight,
Sounds of separators drumming
   In the pale moonlight.
Sounds of dogs, and creaking wagons,
And the heavy smell of grain—
And the call of distant voices
That I'll never hear again.

Index of Poems

First lines of fragments or of verses with no title are in quotation marks.

THE AUTHOR

Paul Hiebert was born in 1892. He grew up in small towns on the prairies, worked on a farm and in a general store, and at one time taught school in a Saskatchewan dust-bowl town. The locale of *Sarah Binks* is derived from these experiences. Hiebert holds the B.A. degree from the University of Manitoba, the M.A. from the University of Toronto, and received his PH.D. from McGill University in Physics and Chemistry. He was Professor of Chemistry at the University of Manitoba when *Sarah Binks* was written. Two years after the publication of his satirical biography he wrote an article entitled "A Chemist Among the Literati" in *Chemistry in Canada* (December, 1949). He has also been heard on the CBC in a program devoted to the life and works of his imaginary heroine.

THE NEW CANADIAN LIBRARY LIST